## "Where did you find it? Have you told the police?"

Gustavo's brain tried to catch up with what Jeannie had just said. The look they had shared was still sending sparks through his system, and he was struggling to understand the sudden shift.

"The police?" he said, wondering if he'd actually heard her correctly.

Jeannie's eyes were sparkling in a way he remembered so well from high school, but what was it about this book that made her look like that?

"They are going to have a field day when they see this," she muttered, staring at the object with disbelief on her face.

"Is it stolen?" he asked, wondering how she could know that from just looking at the inside cover.

"Even better!" she gushed, almost squealing.

"What does that even mean?" Gustavo asked, wondering if she could hear him through the fog of excitement that had clearly taken possession of her.

He was missing a whole lot of pieces to this jigsaw puzzle...

**Ali Olson** is a resident of Bothell, Washington, where she is kept very busy raising three young children, though she still somehow finds a little time to write, and she's very thankful for that. She has loved reading and writing her entire life and is thrilled that she gets to share her words with others. She appreciates hearing from readers. Write to her at authoraliolson.com.

## Books by Ali Olson

### Love Inspired Mountain Rescue

*Trapped at the Summit*

Visit the Author Profile page
at LoveInspired.com for more titles.

# KILLER PAST

## ALI OLSON

**LOVE INSPIRED**
INSPIRATIONAL ROMANCE

Recycling programs for this product may not exist in your area.

ISBN-13: 978-1-335-42614-7

Killer Past

Copyright © 2022 by Mary Olson

For questions and comments about the quality of this book, please contact us at CustomerService@Harlequin.com.

Love Inspired
22 Adelaide St. West, 41st Floor
Toronto, Ontario M5H 4E3, Canada
www.LoveInspired.com

Printed in U.S.A.

Thou shalt not kill.
—*Exodus* 20:13

The thief cometh not, but for to steal, and to kill,
and to destroy: I am come that they might have life,
and that they might have it more abundantly.
—*John* 10:10

And above all things have fervent charity
among yourselves: for charity shall cover
the multitude of sins.
—*1 Peter* 4:8

To my best friends: Blair, Adrianne, and Ian.
I will never be able to express what each of you
means to me. Thank you for everything.

# Chapter One

"Here's the last one," Gustavo Rodriguez said, handing the glitter-covered Santa ornament to Angie, who stretched her two-year-old arms and carefully placed it as high on the large Christmas tree as she could reach.

"All done!" she announced, looking at the tree with the pride of an architect who'd just completed their first skyscraper.

Gustavo smiled at his daughter. She didn't seem to notice that the top half of the tree was totally bare, or that the parts she managed to reach only held the few ornaments he'd bought at the same time he'd gotten the tree. Up until a few days ago, he'd owned exactly zero ornaments, and their collection was still underwhelming, but he would fix that over the next few weeks. He silently vowed that by Christmas it would be weighed down with ornaments, with a beautiful angel gracing the top, and that it wouldn't be standing alone in a nearly empty living room. He would give Angie the best Christmas she could hope for, where she would wake up in her own room and run out to see a beautiful tree surrounded by presents. He wanted her to have the love and the home she deserved.

There was still a long way to go before they got there, he thought, looking around at the bare room and the broken empty bookshelves, which were the only furniture in this part of the house. He ran through his mental list of everything he would need to do over the next few days and weeks. It was daunting, but the furniture would be arriving in a few days and hopefully by Christmas the place would at least be comfortable.

Not that Angie seemed to mind the level of disrepair of the old place. She seemed absolutely delighted by the sheer number of odds and ends left around the house when the aging previous owner moved out. She'd been running up to him shouting, "What this, Papa?" since they'd moved in, after finding a wrench, a spanner and a hunk of leather that he guessed was once part of a saddle, along with several even more strange and unidentifiable objects. She had spent every day since they came here exploring and giggling over every corner of the big house.

Her enthusiasm brought a smile to his face and fed his own excitement. As much work as he had ahead of him, Gustavo thanked God for it. This place was what he'd wanted all these years. A ranch to fix

up and call his own, some land and the little hometown of Colby, Kentucky, that he'd loved so much.
He could feel the past fifteen years slipping off him,
like a weight he'd finally decided to drop.

He heard the front door open and a half-shouted,
"Knock, knock!"

Angie scrambled toward the door with screams
of excitement, her dark curls bouncing along as she
ran. A few seconds later, the girl returned, pulling
Beba—the closest the little one could get to saying
*abuela*—over to see the tree. Gustavo saw the bulg-
ing bag his mother was holding and held in a sigh.
He was grateful for his mother's help and support,
but she seemed to bring a dozen trinkets every single
time she came over, which was very *very* frequently.

As suspected, the bag was quickly emptied, which
created a scattered pile on the floor consisting of
crayons, doll's clothes, a bug collecting kit and some
cube thing which probably did something, though
what it was he had no idea.

The older woman sat on the floor beside her grand-
daughter, laughing as the girl rummaged through the
bag one last time, searching for anything that might
have been missed.

Gustavo kissed the older woman on the cheek.
"*Hola*, Mama. Christmas is still a month away, you
know," he told her, gesturing at the pile of things.

"Oh hush, *mijo*," she said, waving away his con-
cerns. "This little one needs plenty to do until then,

and I'm sure there will be plenty of gifts under the tree for her come Christmas."

Of that he had no doubt. He watched as Angie moved on to examining her haul and pushing buttons on the cube, which apparently was created to make loud cacophonous electronic noises.

Gustavo made a mental note to leave that toy at Beba's house. He looked again at his mother and was still surprised that this woman was the same person who had raised him. He had been so sure she would be disappointed when he gave up his law career and his place in the city to buy a rundown ranch in his hometown, bringing a daughter he'd only just met with him. Instead, she had jumped at the chance to be a part of their life and a real *abuela* to Angie.

In fact, there was very little of the stern woman he'd grown up with left in her. That perpetual frown from his childhood, the sadness in her eyes, had both disappeared, and her dark hair curled messily around her shoulders as she crawled on the floor with the child, no longer in that tight bun he'd come to associate with her. Even the way she called him *mijo* had changed, as if she really felt the affection instead of using the endearment out of maternal duty.

Gustavo hadn't understood his mother when he was young, and he'd never heard her entire story, but he knew enough to be aware that the world hadn't been kind to her and she had expected perfection from him as a way to protect him from discrimination and an unhappy marriage, two things she had battled with for most of her life.

He still wasn't used to this version of her, the one that had only surfaced after her father ran off with a younger woman, and he was nervous that it would fade and she would once again be distant and unforgiving, but she seemed happy and he was grateful for that.

Her desire for perfection did still come out on occasion, however. She looked around his mess of a house and sighed. "This placc is not ready for a child to live yet, *mijo*," she said.

Gustavo suppressed a sigh of his own at needing to repeat the same conversation yet again. "Mama, if we waited for the previous owner's family to clean and repair before we moved in, it would have meant months and thousands more dollars," he said. "I am keeping Angie safe, and this way I get to fix it the way I want it. Just you wait—in two months' time it will be *perfecto*."

"With furniture, *espero*," she added.

"Furniture will arrive any day now," he promised.

She looked skeptical, but then turned her attention to the little girl and her face brightened. She loved the little girl, that much was clear, and after a few days of suspicion, Angie came to trust and love her Beba. She was ecstatic about having a playmate, especially one who brought her so many exciting things, and his mother seemed genuinely happy to have them home, even if she disapproved of their current living conditions.

Angie grabbed the magnifying glass from the bug kit and started examining the floors, searching for insects. Gustavo prayed she wouldn't find any, both because it would add another reason for his mother to shake her head and because he didn't need any more projects.

Angie continued on her search, with *abuela* following close behind, out of the living room and into the bedroom that would eventually be hers once he'd toddler-proofed it, cleared out the junk and figured out how to get the window to latch shut.

So far the only areas in the house that were truly livable were his bedroom—thanks to a borrowed air mattress from his mother—and the kitchen, which he had been determined to have ready to make a Thanksgiving meal on very short notice. His mother had been a little exasperated that he insisted on doing the meal at his new place when she had a comfortable home a few miles away, but it had been important to Gustavo, and the holiday had come off nearly crisis-free. As soon as they had finished the meal, it had been time for a Christmas tree. With that in place, he needed to decide what project to tackle next.

There was so much to do, and he knew it would take a long while and many hours of labor to make this place a real home, but Gustavo could only feel pure joy at the life that stretched ahead for him and Angie. He looked again at the Christmas tree and he listened to the toddler babble from whatever room she was searching through at the moment. He wanted to give Angie the best Christmas of her young life, and his heart filled to see how happy she'd already become.

When Angie's mother brought her to his door a few months ago, demanding that he take the child he hadn't known he'd fathered, the little girl had been quiet and careful, sad and sullen. But as quickly as he'd discovered that this was what was missing from his life, she'd opened up and become an energetic, bubbly little child. It had been almost fifteen years since he'd cared for anyone, and he was determined to make a good life for the two of them.

Angie's squeals of delight and the sound of her tiny running feet approaching brought Gustavo into the present. He waited, desperately hoping she wasn't about to show him a family of termites the inspector missed.

"Book, Daddy, book!" she shouted with glee, running up to him.

He was more than relieved to see that this wasn't a mispronunciation of *bug*, but was, in fact, a book. Before he could do more than take the small leather book from the child's hands, she was off again, the thunder of her tiny feet loud in the bare rooms.

Gustavo was about to set the book on a broken bookshelf, one of his many necessary projects, but something about the item made him pause. He turned it over, studying the worn cover with the embossed letters. It certainly didn't match the other items Angie had discovered around the house. The man who had lived here didn't seem to have been the reading type, and any publications to be found seemed likely to be grabbed near the checkout at the local grocery store and exclusively for bathroom use.

Gustavo read the title: *A Christmas Carol*, by Charles Dickens. He felt a wave of unreality as he opened the front cover and flipped through the pages. As he looked through it, he couldn't help but think of Jeannie Lawson, his high school girlfriend. She was passionately interested in books, or at least had been in high school, and *A Christmas Carol* had been one of her particular favorites.

She had read it at least twice every year between October and December for the entire time he had known her, which added up to more than twenty read-throughs, and the book was indelibly linked to her in his mind. He wondered if she still did that, and hoped so. There was something comforting in the thought that even all these years later, she might be tucking her legs beneath her as she sat on the floor and read the familiar words again and again.

Gustavo tried to dismiss her from his mind as he held the book, his fingers running along the spine. He had tried to forget Jeannie since high school, but she always seemed to crop back up. A million little things reminded him of her, his first—and if he was being honest with himself, his only—love. Little things like this book. Especially now that he'd returned to Kentucky, walking the streets of Colby—their hometown—where they had strolled hand in hand, passing dozens of spots that held special remembrances of her and their time together.

And he had heard just the other day that her mother had passed away, which broke his heart. Mrs. Lawson was one of the loveliest people he'd ever met, and to think that she was no longer in the world, making her suncatchers and helping anybody who crossed her path no matter how little time or money she had to spare, was a devastating thought. He'd wanted to call Jeannie or check on her family, but he doubted he'd be welcome and decided to stay away. Still—

"What is that, *mijo*?" his mother asked from so near that he jumped.

He forced himself back to the present and turned to her, holding up the book and attempting to sound casual. "Angie found this somewhere around the house," he said.

His mother gave him a little smile. "So that's what the girl scampered away with," she said, clearly not quite as innocent as she was attempting to sound. "One of your friends in school used to love that book, no?"

Gustavo was sure his mother knew exactly who. He narrowed his eyes. "Jeannie Lawson," he answered, waiting to see what game she was playing.

She nodded. "*Claro*, Jeannie! I should have remembered. Especially since I saw her this morning at the hardware store," she said casually, as if this wasn't what she'd been planning from the beginning. "I bought some things to childproof our homes, now that there's a little one around," she added, looking up at the bookshelves, as if she knew he needed time to process the fact that she had seen his high school girlfriend earlier that day.

Which was time he certainly needed. Jeannie was here in Colby? For the holiday weekend, or for good? Was it possible the two of them would be living in the same small town, bumping into each other at the hardware store and as they strolled downtown? A hundred questions ran through his mind. He looked at the book.

"Perhaps you should go visit her," the older woman added softly, tapping the book in his hands. "Bring her this and catch up."

He looked at her, suddenly very suspicious. "Did you buy this and bring it here so I would go see her?" he asked.

His mother tried to look offended for a brief moment before giving it up and shrugging. "I would have found some way to get you to go see her, but this was not me. The *niña* found it behind that old chair that belongs in *la basura*."

He decided not to argue about whether or not the chair was trash and instead looked at the book once more.

"God put it there for her to find, I think," she added. "Don't ignore His gift to you, *mijo*. I was not always the kindest to Jeannie when you two were children—I believed you to be too young to know what was good for you—but I see now that she is still your *amor* even after all these years, and here is a reason to see her again. And you must pay your respects to her mother. *Es perfecto.*"

He wasn't sure what to say to that. He hadn't seen Jeannie in so long, but she'd never been far from his thoughts. And the coincidence of Angie discovering this book among the detritus left by the previous owner was too big to disregard.

"Do you want me to watch the little one?" his mother asked.

Gustavo considered that. "No," he said at last. "I'll take her with me."

He was relieved that he didn't need to explain why as his mother nodded and gave him a brief kiss on the cheek. It felt very important to him that Jeannie and Angie meet each other.

"Come here, Angie. We're going to visit a friend," he said, picking her up and carrying her toward the door, tucking the small book into his pocket.

"New friend?" Angie asked.

Gustavo wasn't sure how to answer that as he slipped on his jacket, wondering what Jeannie was or would be to either of them. "New to you, sweetie. I've known her a long time."

Jeannette Lawson was still a little shaken when she got home with groceries and a variety of drill bits, wood screws and other miscellanea, but she tried to push it all away as best she could as she stepped into her childhood home. This wasn't a time to be thinking about her ex-boyfriend, she told herself. She was here in Colby to be with her family when they most needed her.

The noise when she came through the door was nearly overwhelming, but it was the kind of cacophony that made her heart happy. Her nieces and nephew ran by, shouting something about super robots and an emergency in the kitchen. Jeannette stood there, bags in hand, watching them as they disappeared through the doorway of the kitchen. From her sister's muffled shout and the crash that followed, Jeannette guessed that if there hadn't been an emergency before, there certainly was one now.

Before she could follow to help or stand back and laugh, whichever seemed most appropriate when she got there, her father walked into the hallway. "I heard the commotion. Everything okay?"

Jeannette listened for a moment and shrugged. "Based on the level of scolding, I'm guessing it was messy but not dangerous," she replied.

Reassured, Jeannette's father turned his attention to her and engulfed her in a tight hug, as if she'd come home from somewhere much farther than the hardware store. Jeannette's arms, loaded down with groceries, were pinned at her side, but she leaned her head against his shoulder and soaked up his affection.

He'd always been a loving father, but it had ramped

up considerably since her mother passed away a few months before. Or maybe she hadn't been home enough in recent years to notice it.

When he let go, her father was giving her his biggest smile, though she could still see the sadness in his eyes. "I'm so glad you decided to stay through the holidays, sweetie," he told her, putting a hand on her shoulder.

She felt guilty for wanting to run to Seattle and for not being home enough, and she regretted that her mother wasn't there with them. Grief from her mother's death coursed through her, but she pushed it aside as she had every time it threatened to overwhelm her. She couldn't let herself fall apart, especially not in front of her father, who was dealing with his own pain and loss. So instead, she smiled and extricated one paper bag from the rest. "And I come bearing gifts," she said. "I'm like the wise men, if they got their gifts from the local hardware store."

"I wouldn't know what to do with frankincense, anyway," her father replied, taking the proffered bag with glee. "These I can use."

"What are you making in your shed?" she asked, curious.

"Oh you'll see," he said with a silly little wink that made her chuckle. "You better go help your sister," he added, turning away.

Before she could ask any more questions, he was gone, off to do whatever it was he had planned, and Jeannette entered the kitchen. Her sister Beth and the kids were all on their hands and knees with rags, cleaning up a large amount of spilled liquid that seemed to have coated the entire floor. From the overpowering smell of apples, Jeannette guessed that it was cider. She stepped carefully around the mess and set the bags on the counter. Now with her hands free, she grabbed a towel. "Want some help?" she asked.

"Oh no," Beth said, standing up. "They made the mess so they can certainly clean it up."

"We're an emergency robot crew, not a cleaning robot crew!" Stella, the five-year-old, complained, stomping one foot to emphasize her indignation. Rachel and Carson, too old for foot stomping at ages seven and eight, nodded in agreement.

"Well, cleaning this up before it ruins the floors is definitely an emergency," her mother responded calmly. "I'm going to help Aunt Jeannie put away groceries and you three will take care of this, and soon everything will be done and then we can have some lunch. Won't that be nice?"

With her cheerful tone, Jeannette wondered if her sister was going to suggest they all sing "Whistle While You Work," but instead she walked over and gave Jeannette a smirk that showed she knew exactly how saccharine she sounded, and Jeannette had to suppress a chuckle.

The kids continued wiping up the mess—though not without grumbles—as Beth walked over to her sister. "How was your trip into town?" she asked, pulling broccoli from one of the bags on the counter.

Jeannette didn't know how to answer as she, too, began unloading bags. *Fine* felt like a lie after all that had happened. "It was…productive," she finally said.

Beth looked at her while squinting her eyes. "Tell me what happened," she said, folding her arms and waiting for the whole story.

Jeannette sighed. She'd never been able to get anything past her sister, as children or adults. Even though Beth was younger than her by two years, it often felt the other way around. It could be infuriating sometimes. "I bumped into Mrs. Rodriguez. You know, Gustavo's mom," she said.

Beth gave a low whistle. "Gustavo's mom," she repeated, shaking her head. "That's some Ghost of Christmas Past stuff right there. How was that?"

Jeannette found herself once again unsure how to respond. "It was strange," she said. "She was being so friendly, like she was happy to see me. She'd always been so cold before. And she told me Gustavo was moving back to town."

She didn't know where to go from there. The whole interaction had felt surreal, as if it was happening in a different life where she had healed from the past instead of carrying the hurt around, even after all these years.

But Beth didn't seem to need the rest of the story to understand. "Are you going to see him?"

Jeannette shrugged, then said aloud the part that

had been gnawing at her the whole time, as silly as she knew it was after all these years. "He has a family now. His mom was buying things to childproof her house. She was so excited to tell me about her sweet little granddaughter."

"Oof," Beth said, squeezing Jeannette's shoulder before returning to emptying the bags.

Jeannette nodded and followed suit, glad for something to do. *Oof* was about the best way to describe it, and she was grateful that her sister understood.

"Do you think you can put the past behind you now?" Beth said gently.

"It *is* behind me," Jeannette answered automatically. "It was fifteen years ago."

Beth didn't answer, just continued grabbing produce while giving Jeannette a little look that she couldn't read. Her sister seriously frustrated her sometimes.

"I don't know how we're going to live together for the next month," she said, giving Beth a shoulder nudge as they crowded in front of the refrigerator to show she was joking. She hoped Beth would allow the change in subject so they could move away from a topic where she didn't like the answers.

Beth stared at her sister for a long second, then looked over at the three children as they finished their attempt to clean the spill. She sighed, seeming to accept that her sister didn't want to probe into her feelings for Gustavo. "I'm glad Dad still has this big rambling house, so we all fit. I told him and Mom to move years ago, but I'm sure you can guess how that went," she said with a smile.

Jeannette could imagine it perfectly. She'd had the exact conversation with them, and it had gone nowhere. Her parents adored their home, even though it had always been bigger than they really needed or could even afford. She remembered when they were in danger of losing it when she was in high school, and felt that same twinge of guilt she got every time she thought about that sudden influx of money they received her senior year. Still, her parents were able to keep their home and make a few much-needed upgrades, and that was what was important.

Now, with Jeannette, Beth and Beth's three children all staying there, it finally felt like a full house. She only wished her mother was there to experience it. "I can't tell you what a help it is to be with you and Dad right now, with David away," Beth said, throwing an arm around Jeannette and giving her a kiss on the cheek. "You're a Godsend."

Jeannette didn't know about that, but she was happy to be there for her sister while her brother-in-law was on deployment. "I'm glad you could rent out your place and come stay here for a while. I know it means the world to Dad."

Beth smiled and grabbed a rag, and Jeannette followed to help finish the job the kids had half completed. "If my kids don't destroy the entire house before Christmas. He'll probably be more than a little relieved when David comes home in January and he gets some quiet back," Beth said.

"It'll give him another project to do, fixing up everything that gets broken," Jeannette told her. "Speaking of, any idea what he's working on? He asked me to grab a bunch of things from the hardware store but won't tell me what they're for."

Beth shook her head. "All he's told me is that it's a surprise and we need to stay out of his workshop."

Jeannette knelt beside her sister and they cleaned up the last of the spill shoulder to shoulder, and she felt herself relax a little, reveling in the feeling of home. There was so much she didn't know, but the love she felt for her family was absolute, and that was a comfort.

A few minutes later, the spill was clean, the groceries were away and Beth was busy serving up lunch. Jeannette held a stack of forks out to her littlest niece, kneeling and looking the girl in the eye. "Do you think you can get these on the table, kiddo?" she asked in the same way she would ask the girl to carry priceless and fragile artifacts.

Stella nodded, just as serious as her aunt, and carefully took the pile of silverware. She walked with all the care of someone holding precious objects, taking tiny steps toward the dining room. Jeannette's heart swelled at the sight.

"She's great, isn't she?" Beth whispered, watching her daughter walk ever so slowly to her destination.

"They all are," Jeannette said, standing and wrapping an arm around her sister. "You made some pretty amazing kids."

"It's not easy when David's gone. I really appreciate you and Dad helping me out," Beth said, resting her head on Jeannette's shoulder.

Jeannette rarely saw her sister vulnerable, and it did her heart good to feel like she was being a decent big sister when Beth needed her. They stood there together for a few moments and Jeannette soaked it all in.

She hadn't admitted to herself how much she missed her family while living alone up in Washington State and only seeing them for a few days a couple times a year. She'd been so focused on getting her career going in the right direction that she hadn't let herself think about it much, but now that she was here, she felt a weight on her shoulders fall away, one she hadn't even realized was there. She promised God she would be a better aunt and sister and daughter.

Jeannette loved her nieces and nephew, and she was excited to spend an entire month in her childhood home with them. Even though she worried about her career and desperately wanted to avoid seeing Gustavo again after so many years, she knew this was an opportunity to bond with these kids in a way she couldn't when she was hardly ever around. And it made her wonder if perhaps she was missing something, staying so focused on work that she'd managed to avoid any opportunity to have a family of her own. A family like the one Gustavo now apparently had. Her heart squeezed tight and she focused on the family she *did* have: her dad and sister and these three little ones.

A part of her was going to be very sad to leave, despite how important it was for her to return. Financially, though, it was really the only choice. She'd worked too hard to get to this spot to have a big setback now. She had to hope that this month off wouldn't ruin everything. She started mentally running through the ad campaigns they were working on and what she would need to do when she returned to Seattle. Maybe if she took some time here and there to do a few things, she wouldn't be so far behind when she got back, as unappealing as that sounded. She would probably have time to—

"You're thinking about work again, aren't you?" Beth asked, cutting into Jeannette's thoughts as she tilted her head to look up at her sister.

Jeannette laughed. "How did you know?"

"You always get tense when you're thinking about your job," Beth answered, moving away to grab plates. "Honestly, you better be careful or the stress is going to give you an ulcer."

Jeannette couldn't argue with that. The number of nights she woke up worried and anxious, the number of days she had to drag herself through, was a problem, to say the least. It was all worth it, though, she reminded herself.

"I remember how much you loved completing your

community service hours at the library, and your time working at the university. You can't tell me this job is better than that?"

Jeannette couldn't. "Those were kid jobs—community service and experience—but they paid hardly anything. If I had wanted to work there, I would've needed to get a degree in Library Science and I still would've made a fraction of what I do on one ad campaign," she explained to her sister.

Beth didn't look convinced. "Do you *enjoy* your job, Jeannie? Even a little? Tell the truth," she said, looking at Jeannette with serious, concerned eyes.

Jeannette suddenly felt like she was the little child being given an important task, that her sister expected something from her, but she didn't know how to respond in a way that wouldn't cause Beth to give her some kind of motherly lecture, possibly accompanied by a seriously exasperated finger point. It was true; she missed her hours spent working in libraries throughout high school and college, all the enjoyment she'd gotten from cataloguing pieces and repairing texts, and she'd daydreamed about changing her major and later her career. But marketing was lucrative and that mattered, too, even if it wasn't her passion.

She didn't want to barely get by, like her parents had for all those years.

She didn't think Beth would agree with her, though, and it didn't sound like an argument Jeannette particularly wanted to have right at that moment. Fortunately, her nephew Carson rushed into the kitchen at that moment, saving her from needing to reply and giving her an excuse to look away from that piercing gaze. At eight, Carson seemed to be always in a hurry, and this moment was no different. "Aunt Jeannie, there's some man at the door for you!" he said breathlessly.

"Who—" Jeannette started, but before she could finish the question, Carson was gone, dashing off to whatever other task needed his attention. Jeannette didn't really need to ask, though. She knew the only man it could possibly be.

Gustavo had come to visit.

# Chapter Two

Jeannette let out a little sigh. She had hoped Gustavo's mother would keep their encounter to herself, but clearly she hadn't, and Gustavo must have decided not to waste any time. That might have made her feel a little nervous, or perhaps confused. But knowing he had a family, that he'd moved on with his life, made her as desperate to avoid him as she'd been fifteen years ago, when she'd left home hoping to never see him again.

Except he was here, standing at her front door right that minute, and there was nothing she could do.

Beth gave her an encouraging smile and made a shooing motion toward the door. "It'll be fine. You better go and let him in. I'm sure he's standing awkwardly outside the door where Carson left him."

Jeannette sighed and nodded, reluctantly leaving the kitchen. As she walked across the living room toward the front door, she very much wished she were in the kitchen with Beth having that awkward conversation about her job. Or, better yet, helping the noisy kids in the dining room and avoiding all the discomfort altogether.

But it was too late. Gustavo was here whether she wanted it or not, so she crossed into the front hall and looked toward the open door where he stood. He looked as handsome as ever—tall with dark hair curling around his ears, perhaps a little older but with that same kind, piercing expression, which at that moment was focused on the little girl in his arms. She had a mass of her own dark curls framing a sweet little face. The young female version of him. She was chattering away, and Gustavo watched her as if he was enthralled with everything the child said.

Jeannette's heart ached so much it was difficult to breathe. It was more than obvious that Gustavo adored his daughter, and part of her wondered what might have been. What if they'd had a child, if she'd had that experience with him…

Jeannette reined in her thoughts, mentally telling herself to stop it, to get ahold of herself. Thinking about what could have been made the reality harder to handle, and she reminded herself that she was happy with her own life. It was one she'd chosen, and she was doing perfectly well, thank you very much. *He* was the one who had decided not to be with her fifteen years ago, the one who had drifted away with no explanation, and no matter how handsome he was and how sweetly he looked at his daughter, she wouldn't want to be with someone who would do that. It was better this way. She said a quick prayer for strength and walked the last few feet to the door.

"Gustavo," she said by way of a greeting. "Your mother told you I was in town?"

She knew she probably didn't sound too kind, but she couldn't figure out how to forgive him for moving on and finding happiness without her, and never telling her why. And then bringing this adorable little girl over, as if to show her the future she had lost. Her hurt and confusion was hardening into anger fast.

"Hi, Jeannie," he answered, sounding almost embarrassed. "Yeah, she said she saw you."

Jeannette waited, watching as the little girl held a large magnifying glass to her eye, looking all the world like a very adorable Sherlock Holmes. If Jeannette hadn't felt quite so heartsore and irritated at this emotional intrusion into her life, she would've melted as the little girl examined her so carefully, her eye appearing huge through the glass.

Jeannette was ready to tell Gustavo that this was a bad time—that she was about to sit down to lunch and he should probably leave—but then he held up a small book and the words fell away. "We found this at my new place, and I thought you might like it," he said, looking uncomfortable.

As much as she didn't want to care about this thing he'd found, she couldn't help but reach for it. Her fingers accidentally brushed against his as it passed between them, and for a moment Jeannette felt a wave of nostalgia and those old emotions rush through her, but she clamped down on those feelings, reminding herself that all that was in the long-distant past. Annoyed at her curious nature, Jeannette looked at what he'd brought. The moment she saw what it was, though, she had to smile. *"A Christmas Carol,"* she murmured, wondering at the coincidence of Beth's earlier comment.

"We found this," he said, sounding like he knew exactly how lame the repetition sounded, "and I know it looks pretty ratty, but it made me think of you," he finished awkwardly.

It had been years since she'd read the story, and her heart squeezed tight when she thought of the times she'd sat with Gustavo, reading it aloud to him and doing ridiculous voices for the characters while their legs crossed over each other.

She softened a little. "Would you like to come in for a minute?" she said, glancing behind him nervously in search of his female counterpart.

When he stepped in, though, she was relieved to see that it was just him and the girl. She didn't know how she would have gotten through meeting his wife, and she thanked God for that favor. They all went into the living room, Jeannette clutching the book tight in her hands.

She thought again of Beth's "Ghost of Christmas Past" comment and wondered if God was trying to tell her something.

She put that aside and led the two guests into the

living room, though she was sure Gustavo would still know the way well enough on his own. He had been there enough times when they were kids; he could probably walk through the house blindfolded.

As Jeannette showed him into the house, she saw it through his eyes—how it had changed since the last time he'd been there. The upgraded furniture, newish carpet. Very different from the thrift shop chic her family used to sport when she was a kid, embarrassing her to no end.

Back then, when they were preteen friends studying together, she hadn't wanted to invite him inside, and it had taken her a long time to overcome that particular hurdle. She hadn't liked any of her friends coming over. At that time, she'd been embarrassed with anybody seeing her home, but especially Gustavo.

Not because she thought he would make fun of her, but because of how different it was from the nice house he lived in. She had envied that beautiful house with all its nice furniture, and she didn't want him to see how differently she lived. When they first started dating as sophomores, she struggled with that even more than she had before. She didn't want to remind him of how mismatched they were, afraid that one day he'd wake up and realize her family was too poor for him. She had seen it in his mother's eyes enough to know it was true. Her kindness earlier that day had seemed strange at first, but Jeannette now understood that Mrs. Rodriguez no longer needed to worry about her son marrying a poor woman. He was taken, and she seemed more than pleased about it.

Jeannette had always feared at least a little that her poverty was the reason he'd distanced himself, but the timing didn't fit, and it never exactly sat right. It was only when her parents were doing okay that he started to step away. And whatever his mother's feelings were, Gustavo had never hinted at her family and their house being anything but wonderful. Still, those years of embarrassment had been difficult to overcome, no matter what he said.

Now, though, she wasn't embarrassed about this house. It still didn't look like the house of a wealthy family and never would, but at least it looked like the people who lived here were comfortable enough to get by. Nobody here would need to pinch pennies at the end of the month or pull out yet another jar of preserved vegetables to make it through the winter. Or feel guilty for bringing home a field trip form that required a few dollars to go.

Her parents always found the money, but the look on their faces was always so hard to see.

She brought herself back to the present and gestured to the couch, where Gustavo sat, holding his daughter on his lap and looking around at the changes. As she watched, an expression flashed across his face that she didn't expect, and it gave her pause. It looked almost like disappointment.

She wondered why he would feel disappointed,

looking around at her old home, where they had spent so much time together. Her heart couldn't help but chime in that maybe he regretted how they ended, too. But as quickly as she registered it, the expression was gone.

For a second she considered asking him about the look he had and delving into that mystery of the past, but finally she decided to let the moment go without comment. Even if he wished things had been different, he'd made his choice and it no longer mattered, anyway. He had a family and she had her own life to live very far away from his.

So she instead turned her attention to the thin novel in her hands. She forced her eyes to stay on the book, even though she felt him watching her. "Thank you," she said again, for lack of anything better to say. She opened the front cover. "I haven't—"

Her words died in her mouth. She flipped through the pages, felt the edges and examined the cover. She dropped to the floor, where she always felt a bit more comfortable than the couch, and which felt farther from Gustavo's uncomfortable presence. She touched the front again, her fingers feeling the slightly bumpy surface, then opened it once more, very delicately this time, and ran her fingers along the inside cover.

As she looked at it, her face moved nearer and nearer to the page so she could see every minute detail, down to the bleed of the ink. Memories rushed through her. She couldn't believe it, but there it was, staring her in the face.

She didn't even realize that Gustavo's daughter was no longer on his lap, but was instead standing right next to her and watching through her magnifying glass. So when Jeannette finally sat up straight and felt someone so close to her, she gave a little yelp.

"Sorry about that," Gustavo said, pulling his daughter back a few inches to give Jeannette a little space.

"I am exploring lots of hair!" the girl explained. "For bugs!"

Jeannette looked to Gustavo for some explanation. He seemed to be trying very hard not to laugh at the scene in front of him. "She's a budding entomologist," he told her with the shrug of a father who had a child too small to understand things like personal space.

Jeannette turned to the little girl, who seemed to never get tired of holding up her magnifying glass. "Sorry, there are no bugs in my hair," Jeannette told her, almost wishing that this wasn't true when she saw the disappointment on the child's face.

After a moment, though, the child regrouped and turned her attention to the carpet, crawling along in her search, almost looking like a bug herself. Jeannette watched her for a moment, fascinated by this tiny person. She looked up at Gustavo and they shared a smile that warmed her through to her toes.

And then she felt the pain and anger that burned so deeply and returned her attention to the object in her hand to get away from those emotions. She couldn't let herself get caught up in those things when something much more important was right in her hands.

Her heart sped up, but not for the same reason it did when she looked at Gustavo. The more she looked at the book, the surer she was that this was something very special, and she knew exactly what that was.

"This is amazing," she told him at last, holding up the classic with a surprised shake of her head. "Where did you find it? Are there any more? Have you told the police?"

Gustavo's brain tried to catch up with what Jeannie had just said. The look they had shared was still sending sparks through his system, and he was struggling to understand the sudden shift. Even if he hadn't been distracted, he didn't think what she was saying would have made any sense.

"The police?" he asked, wondering if he'd actually heard her correctly and hoping she would tell him that of course this book wasn't *that* interesting.

But Jeannie's eyes were sparkling in a way he remembered so well from high school, and he knew that it was exactly that interesting to her. It was the same look she'd have on her face when she needed to gush about some wonderful new idea she'd had, some problem she had finally solved. He had no idea what it was about this book that made her look like that, though, or why the police would want to see it.

"They are going to have a field day when they see this," she muttered, staring almost lovingly at the object, opening it again as if to assure herself that it was actually real.

"It's stolen?" he guessed, wondering how she could know that from just looking at it for a few minutes. She knew a lot about books, but even so, that seemed impossible.

"It's even better!" she gushed, almost squealing. She pushed her bug-free hair away from her face as she leaned close to the book again, examining one page after another.

"What does that even mean?" Gustavo asked, wondering if she could hear him through the fog of excitement that had clearly taken possession of her. He was missing a lot of pieces to this jigsaw puzzle, and hoped at some point she would calm down enough to tell him.

She seemed to realize that he needed more information and turned back to the inside cover, passing it into his hands. "Look here," she said, sliding her index finger along the crease where the cover met the first page.

Gustavo looked and didn't see anything, but Jeannie seemed so sure that there was something there, so he brought the book close to his face, searching more carefully, and finally noticed a bit of what appeared to be a frayed edge running along, deep in the crease. "The binding is breaking?" he asked.

"There's a page cut out," she said, taking the book back and running her finger gently along the spot. "It was done very carefully, so you can only tell if you're really paying attention. It really isn't noticeable at all," she added, as if proud of the workmanship.

He waited for more information, but Jeannie seemed to be lost in her own thoughts, unaware that he was still perplexed. "And the person cut out a page because…" he prompted.

"Because they didn't want anyone to see the copyright date," she answered, as if that was the obvious answer.

"So they stole the copyright page," Gustavo said, more confused than ever.

Jeannie shook her head at the guess, but was lost in her own mind as she examined the book more, her nose almost touching the page. Gustavo waited, knowing her well enough to be sure she'd get around to explaining herself eventually. And, as confused and curious as he was, he truly loved seeing her like this, so focused that she hardly knew what was happening around her.

It was the way she'd always gotten when she was particularly fascinated with something, and it had always been something to behold. Her brain moved so quickly sometimes that she forgot others weren't automatically seeing whatever it was she saw. It frustrated some people, but he loved seeing the passion and enthusiasm that she had for the mysteries of the world. And apparently this was one of them.

Finally, she seemed to come out of herself enough to realize he was still staring at her. When she looked up at him from her spot on the floor, he raised his eyebrows and gave her a patient smile, which finally seemed to get her to register that she wasn't explaining things very clearly. She leaned back a little and tapped the page in front of her. "This book isn't old—" she began, but a voice from the hallway cut her off.

"Jeannie, lunch is on the table," said another woman, leaning into the living room. "Hi, Gustavo," she added with a smile.

It took Gustavo only a second to recognize Jeannie's younger sister as a fully grown adult. He hadn't seen her since she was sixteen, but she had always been so grown up that she looked like she'd hardly changed at all.

He stood and gave her a quick hug. "Beth! It's been a long time," he told her, remembering all the time they'd spent, the three of them, in that very room—playing card games or watching TV or talking about life.

"It really has!" she agreed, a note of wistfulness in her voice.

It was so good to see her again. She had never been "Jeannie's annoying little sister," just a part of the group, and he had missed her. Had missed the entire family.

"I was so sorry to hear about your mom," he said, wishing words could better express how he felt. Their mother had truly been a wonderful woman. "I hope your dad is doing okay."

Beth shrugged, her grief evident on her face for only a moment before it became conversational and pleasant. "He's happy to have us home," she told Gustavo.

The women in this family had always been strong, but he wondered if either of them had let themselves really grieve their mother's passing or if they'd both simply pushed it to the side in order to take care of what needed to be done.

Gustavo hoped they were taking time for themselves while they were home with their father, but then he heard what sounded like a dozen children in the dining room, which made him doubt that was even possible. There was so much chattering and clanging of dishes and silverware that he was surprised he hadn't noticed any of it before.

He had met one child when they opened the door, but clearly there had to be more than that one to make so much noise, and it suddenly occurred to him for the first time that Jeannie might be married with several children of her own. A feeling of loss rushed through him at the idea. He knew it was silly, that they'd been apart for fifteen years and certainly weren't getting back together at this point, but the thought still made him ache.

Beth winced at the sounds coming from the other room. "I need to get in there while Dad still has a few plates that aren't broken," she told him, gesturing toward the dining room.

Before leaving, though, she turned to where Jeannie still sat on the floor. "Jeannie?" she asked, giving her sister a significant glance Gustavo very easily read. Beth was trying to give Jeannie the chance to either invite him to stay to eat or tell him it was time to leave, and Beth's protective attitude toward her big sister was evident in every line of her face.

Clearly she was willing to be friendly, but she was also ready to help her sister in any way she could, including very kindly telling Gustavo to leave.

Which was fair. He was sure he hadn't come across too well at the end of his relationship with Jeannie, and to barge in here after all these years right at lunchtime, he certainly didn't deserve or expect an invitation.

He honestly didn't know if he would like to be invited, anyway. If Jeannie had a husband and kids somewhere, maybe seeing them would finally help him get closure on this relationship he'd never managed to get over. Or maybe it would open old wounds even more.

Gustavo walked over to where Angie was still searching, picked her up and gave her a hug. "We should probably get going," he said to the room at large, making it easy on Jeannie. He desperately wanted to know what she was so excited about, but he'd already imposed enough, and he was certain she didn't want him sticking around for lunch. "I just wanted to give you the book," he said as an explanation.

"There are no bugs here," Angie told him, more disappointed than ever.

"Don't leave," Jeannie said, as if that idea was preposterous. "We need to talk about this. Maybe your... daughter would like something to eat while we discuss what you found?" she asked, glancing at Beth, who stepped farther into the room.

Gustavo wondered about the little pause, but Angie was wriggling in his arms and demanding his attention. "I hungry, Papa! Want crackers!" she said.

Beth chuckled and spoke to the little girl with the practiced voice of a mom. "We don't have crackers, but we have yummy chicken drumsticks and carrots and bread I made myself."

Angie seemed a little skeptical about the not-cracker-centric food, but decided she was willing to give it a try. Gustavo set her down and she went with Beth into the dining room, leaving Gustavo and Jeannie alone together.

"Come sit here," Jeannie said to him as soon as the others had gone, sounding exactly like a teacher calling over a student. She pointed to the floor next to her.

Gustavo folded himself into the space on the floor she had indicated, ready for whatever lesson she was about to give and trying not to smile too much at her behavior. She was so engrossed in what they were doing she seemed to have forgotten they were no longer high school sweethearts, and he expected her to swat him any minute for having a smart-aleck smirk on his face, exactly as she used to whenever he was amused by her. Just the reminder of those days made him want to laugh and grimace all at the same time.

He tried to forget about the noise from the other room and about the past and focus on what Jeannie found so interesting.

"This book has been doctored," she began, running her hands carefully over the cover, as if it was an incredibly precious object. "This has been worked to look like old leather—see, if you look closely you can see the scuffs from sandpaper—and the copyright page is gone, and the edges of the rest of the pages have been roughed up to look irregular, like they haven't come out of a modern printing machine. It's not a perfect job, not professionally done, but it's a decent facsimile, good enough to fool anyone who was just glancing at it. Did you find any little tools near it?"

Gustavo remembered the sandpaper Angie had found, as well as the other object in his pocket. He pulled out the small white object. She grabbed it eagerly. "Yes! This is a bone folder," she explained. "You use it to fix books. Or in this case, carefully break books."

Gustavo thought about all this information, trying to understand what Jeannie had seemed to figure out from it and what it could mean. "So somebody wanted to make it look older than it was," he said. She nodded enthusiastically, and he felt like he was catching on a little. "Were they going to sell it as a rare antique?" he asked.

Jeannie shook her head. "No, that would be a stupid thing for them to do. They could get caught, and no matter where down the line the counterfeit got noticed, it could get traced back to whoever did it. I think somebody wanted this book to look just good enough to switch with an *actual* rare version of the same book," she said.

Memories flooded Gustavo as he understood what she meant, and he watched her, his eyes wide with shock. Jeannie didn't seem to notice the change in him—as she was still flipping through the book, closely scanning pages—and continued without looking up at him. "Do you remember our senior year of high school, when the Google team was at the rare books library at the University of Kentucky and I was doing community service and work experience there? They were scanning the collection and discovered that some of them had been stolen and replaced with fakes? This is *exactly* the same as those fake versions. One of the librarians told me all about them and this is identical. I suspect whoever made this planned to steal the real one and put this in its place when they stole the others, but somehow instead it ended up wherever you found it."

Gustavo kept watching her in complete disbelief, suddenly feeling all those old emotions from their senior year. She glanced up and seemed to think he was confused.

"You might not remember it even happened, but I sure do. It wasn't a huge deal to anyone outside of the library, but to us, it was a shock and a lot of work, checking every book for authenticity. I never got to see one of the replicas close up, though. Until now," she said with a smile. "At the time, I'd thought about how cool it would be if I somehow helped to catch the bad guys and return the books to their rightful home, like some kind of superhero who helps novels in distress. And now here you are with something that could really lead to them finally being discovered!"

Gustavo didn't know what to say as he studied her face, which was filled with excitement over a clue to the long-unsolved crime. She seemed to think he had hardly been aware of the theft when it happened, but that was far from the truth. Of course he remembered those stolen books. They had changed the entire path of his life. And now, the way Jeannie was talking about them, he realized what a horrible mistake he had made all those years ago. The truth was crashing in on him and he could only stare at her and try to make sense of the whole thing.

"Gustavo, are you okay?" she asked, looking concerned, as if perhaps she had done something wrong.

Her worry broke his paralysis, and the shame engulfed him. After what he'd done, for her to be kind was so much more than he deserved. He put his hand over his eyes, shaking his head at his own stupidity. "I'm so sorry, Jeannie," he said, his voice raspy with emotion.

He couldn't see her, but he could hear the confusion in her voice when she asked, "Why are you sorry?"

He took a deep breath, thinking through those miserable months all those years ago. What he'd put them both through when he drew his own conclusions and never told her. She deserved to know the truth about what had happened. Gustavo asked God for courage and finally told her the secret he'd been carrying for fifteen years. "Back in high school I—I thought *you* had been the one who stole those books."

## Chapter Three

Jeannette didn't think she'd heard him correctly, but he didn't say anything more to clarify things. She went over it again in her head, but it sounded absolutely crazy and her brain wasn't able to process the words. "You thought I stole those books?" she asked, waiting for him to explain it in a way that made sense.

He looked at her and she could see the anguish in his expression. "You worked there when the books were stolen, and you had been disappointed in their security since that middle school field trip. I remembered how you talked about how easy it would be to take one of those rare books…" he trailed off, looking embarrassed.

Jeannette remembered that field trip. It was one she had desperately wanted to go on, so much so that it was worth seeing the worried expression on her parents' faces. And then when she was there, she noticed there were no cameras or guards in the rare books section of the library and had gotten frustrated that someone could so easily steal one of those books if they wanted to. She'd even come up with the idea of replacing them with fakes so nobody would notice.

And that was when she finally started to understand. But she still couldn't quite grasp the idea that when the books were stolen, his immediate conclusion was that she was a thief. She leaned away from him, feeling anger start to bubble up as it all set in. "You really thought I could do something like that?" she asked, astonished and insulted. She waited for him to explain himself.

"I knew you hated being poor, and I knew money suddenly appeared around here from a surprise oil find on land your parents owned a share of that they didn't even know they had, right at that same time," he said. "Your parents didn't question that, but I saw your expression when they told me about it. You were hiding something—that was obvious—and you changed after that. You pulled away from me because of it. You wouldn't talk to me anymore, not like you had," he continued in a rush, as if these were words he had wanted to say for years. "You seemed ashamed of the money, not excited, and I knew you well enough to know something was wrong about that."

Jeannette felt embarrassment rush through her. He was right—about everything but her stealing those books. She'd been embarrassed about the money, she'd hidden the truth from everyone and she hadn't realized how much she'd changed because of it, but she could see now that it had been enough to ruin her relationship with Gustavo.

"I kept hoping you would tell me the truth eventually," he continued. "I waited, figuring you had a good reason, and I had known you long enough to be aware that sometimes you don't want to share everything going on with you."

Jeannette was about to argue, but kept her mouth shut. The evidence for his statement was too obvious to ignore.

"And then the book theft was discovered and you buried yourself in the investigation. You had changed so much, I had to wonder if you were part of it, working there and everything, and that was where the money came from," he said, looking around at the house her family had almost lost before that sudden influx of cash.

Jeannette felt a sting of shock as she saw how everything lined up. It made so much sense—now that she'd heard the whole story—that he'd concluded that she was a book thief. She hadn't seen it before, never considered how everything could look to someone who didn't know the truth, but there it was. She *had* talked about how simple it would be to steal from the university's rare books collection after their middle school field trip, and she was working at the library at the time, and her family had gotten enough money to stay afloat when they needed it the most. And she had lied. It was too much for her brain to process when she saw it through his eyes.

"I put the pieces together and everything fit," he continued. "I didn't know for sure, but I didn't trust you and you didn't talk to me, and our relationship fell apart," he finished softly.

The long silence felt heavy between them as she gathered herself back together. There was so much there that had finally been said, and so much more that still needed to be. The secrets had been carried like weights on both of them for too long.

"I didn't steal those books," Jeannie said. Her voice was sad and firm, but she could not look anywhere but at the object resting in her hands. She finally understood what had happened—why their relationship had faltered, why all their plans for the future fell apart—but the knowledge brought her no peace. She wasn't sure if it was worse to wonder or to know.

Gustavo's hand twitched, and for a moment she thought he might take one of hers, but then it went still. "I wish I'd been smart enough to talk to you," he said. "If I hadn't been too scared to hear the truth, we wouldn't be in this mess."

Jeannette didn't blame him. Not anymore. She still had her secrets to tell, and she knew how scary it was to share, but she realized that after all these years they needed to move past all the secrets and the wondering.

"What were you hiding from me, Jeannie?" Gustavo asked, sounding like the disappointed teenager he must have been.

Jeannie took a deep breath and prayed to God for strength. She knew none of this mattered now, but it still felt shameful deep down, something she'd never told anyone. She looked around again to make sure nobody would hear them. She couldn't let her dad know what she'd done, even after all this time. "I went to see my uncle," she said at last.

Gustavo wrinkled his forehead, clearly not expecting that answer. "Why would you hide that from me?" he asked, sounding more confused than ever.

Jeannette sighed, remembering that time all those years ago. "He and my dad…never really got along," she explained, speaking softly. "They hadn't talked in years at that point, and he had made it clear that he thought my mother wasn't good enough for the family and my father had made bad choices. It was a mess. But I also knew he had a lot of money and owned a couple of businesses, and my parents thought they might lose the house."

She knew this was the time to tell the truth, so she didn't let herself hold in the rest. "And I needed money for college and was just so tired of being poor. So I found him and begged for help, even though I knew my dad would be furious if he ever found out. I asked for a job, for a handout, for anything he could do for us."

She paused, but after a moment she went on. "He said no. Said my father was lazy and told me I probably wouldn't make it in college anyway. I was so frustrated and upset and ashamed about the whole thing, I couldn't tell anyone, even you. And then the money came in, and I suppose it must have been from him somehow, and I knew how my dad would feel if he found out and I was so embarrassed that I'd begged for it behind everyone's back. I guess that affected me more than I knew."

"So the oil money your parents got, was that from him?" Gustavo asked at last.

Jeannette shrugged. It had been a question she'd asked herself many times over the years. "I honestly don't know. Dad knew he'd been willed land by my great-grandfather. My uncle could easily have been the one to get an oil company interested in leasing it. But he'd been so mean. It's hard to imagine that of him. And even harder to think I was indebted to him after all he'd put my family and me through. So I never looked into it and hoped it was God's doing and nobody else's."

There was a brief silence while they processed all the information they had shared over the past few minutes. Then Jeannette looked up at Gustavo, their eyes meeting with mutual understanding and forgiveness. With everything that had been holding them apart finally torn away, her heart remembered what it was like to be held tight in his arms, and for just a moment she wondered if it could be that way again.

Then Angie ran into the room shouting, "Papa, Papa! I ate carrots like a bunny!"

She trotted to where Gustavo was sitting on the floor and threw her body into his arms, knocking him against the couch. He gripped his daughter in a tight hug and smiled at her, and Jeannette's imagined future evaporated. She'd forgotten that he already had a family, that it was too late for the truth between them to really matter.

And anyway, there was something more interesting to think about. "So, you need to get this book to the police station. Maybe it can help them figure out who the thief was and finally solve the case after all these years."

Jeannette, who had been gripping *A Christmas Carol* the entire conversation, held the book toward him, but only glanced at Gustavo out of the corner of her eye as he stood and took it. She was feeling a little too vulnerable to look at him straight on. He seemed to hesitate as he grasped it, and before she could turn away and show him and his daughter to the door, Gustavo said, "Would you come with me? You know more than I do about all of this. More than anyone at the police station knows, too, I bet. Especially after all these years. It probably won't take too much of your time. I'll need to drop Angie off with my mom and we can go right over."

Jeannette didn't know what to say. Of course she wanted to go to the police and tell them about the book and try to help solve a cold case, like in a movie or something. But she knew it was probably best for her heart to stay out of it and away from Gustavo altogether.

Except he said he wanted to drop Angie off with his mom, not his wife, and this piqued her curiosity almost as much as the book did.

Before she knew that she'd decided, she was nodding and his face lit up with a smile that warmed her heart. "I'll let Beth know," she said, walking toward the kitchen and wondering what, exactly, she would be telling her sister.

Jeannette's nieces and nephew were piling dirty dishes by the sink, while Beth was directing the operation. When she saw Jeannette had entered the room, Beth left the children to their task and walked over, confusion on her face. "What was all that about?" she asked.

"Gustavo and I need to take a book to the police station," Jeannette said, not realizing what a strange sentence that was until it was out of her mouth.

"What crime did the book commit?" Beth asked with raised eyebrows. "Violently split infinitives?"

Jeannette laughed. She gave her sister the briefest of explanations and Beth grinned. "A mystery! How exciting! Have fun investigating crime."

Jeannette shook her head. "We're just taking it to the police station. That's all," she insisted.

Beth didn't seem convinced. "I know you well enough by now, Jeannette Marie, to doubt that you're going to just hand over the book to the police and be done with it."

Jeannette felt the pull to find out everything she could and dive into this puzzle, but it was a police matter and she didn't think there was much she could do, anyway.

She left the kitchen and met Gustavo by the front door, where he was standing watching his daughter as she continued her bug search. Jeannette slipped on her shoes and a jacket, wondering where the girl's mother was.

She tried to tell herself that even if Gustavo was single, too much time had passed for her to hope something could happen between them again, but she couldn't stop a tiny spark of hope from lighting up inside her.

Gustavo had some difficulty focusing on the road as he drove the familiar path from the Lawson home to his childhood residence. With Jeannette beside him in the truck, it felt like old times, except for the chattering coming from the toddler in the rear. He couldn't believe everything that had been revealed in such a short visit, and his mind went back to the book. Could it really be the key to solving a fifteen-year-old mystery? He trusted Jeannie's judgment, but it was all so unlikely.

It was unlikely that a tiny girl would be dropped on his doorstep and change his entire life, though, and that had happened. God was working in his life, and he just needed to have faith that it was all part of the Divine plan.

He certainly wasn't going to complain about being brought together with Jeannie, and he allowed himself to soak in the feel of her sitting beside him again after all these years.

When they reached his mom's house, Gustavo took Angie out of her car seat and carried her to the door. "You're going to stay with Beba for a little while, sweetie," he told her as he opened the door, knocking as they entered.

Angie wriggled out of his arms, excitement on her face. "Beba toys! Beba toys!"

Gustavo smiled as she ran into the house, heading for all the noisiest toys Beba had given the little girl, and he congratulated himself when the sound of tiny hands banging the keys on a little piano filled the air. He wasn't a perfect parent, but keeping the piano at his mom's house had been genius, if he said so himself.

His mom walked into the hallway, her smile bright and seemingly unperturbed by the cacophony, and Gustavo briefly told her what was happening. "You are very sure, Mama, that you found the book inside the house? It is important we know where it came from when we speak to the police."

His mother nodded, serious. "The book was behind that little green chair left in the second bedroom. Angie and I moved it in our search for bugs."

Gustavo accepted this and gave her a hug. "Be

careful, *mijo*," his mother told him, her face looking worn and tired. "Police aren't always our friends."

He could see the old worries in her face, her fear of being treated differently because of their darker skin, and Gustavo hugged his mother tight. "It will be okay, *Mama*. I'll be back soon to get Angie. Thanks for watching her."

He stepped out the door, cool winter air swirling around him as he walked over to the truck where Jeannie was sitting, her face bent over the book once again.

"Find out anything new?" he asked as he climbed into his seat.

Jeannie shook her head. "Nothing new, but it's fascinating. Who did this? Why did they steal those books?"

Gustavo thought for a moment as he pulled onto the street. "Maybe it was just like you noticed on that field trip. It was easy to do, it could make someone a little money and that was enough reason."

Jeannette didn't answer, and they drove the rest of the short distance to the Colby police station in silence. He watched her out of the corner of his eye as she switched between analyzing the book and staring out the window, lost in thought. He had the urge to stop the car and stare at her, soak as much of her in as he could. Seeing her after all these years felt like water after wandering in a desert.

They pulled into the police station parking lot, and

Gustavo parked and cut the engine. He looked over and saw the disappointment on Jeannie's face, and he knew she hated handing over the book and the mystery to the police. The investigators might ask her a couple of questions, but odds were high she would never hear anything else about it again, and he knew how excited she was about this case. He almost suggested they leave and attempt this on their own, but knew that would be wrong.

Still, he couldn't be the one to tell her to give up this case, so he waited patiently for her.

After a minute, Jeannie sighed. "Let's head in," she said.

Gustavo and Jeannette walked into the police station. Jeannette looked at the book in her hands, and she got the sudden urge to turn around. She wanted to solve this problem on her own—or with Gustavo's help, though the emotions that came with that thought were confusing and she didn't want to think too hard about that. Just holding this book and realizing what it was made her feel alive for the first time in so long. She wanted to chase that feeling and any clues she could find and see where it all would take her. Her life and career in Seattle never gave her this feeling, this fire inside her, and it was going to be hard to let it go and walk away.

But it was the right thing to do, she knew. The police had resources and authority and the right to investigate this case. She didn't. So she turned her eyes to the front desk, ready to greet the officer standing there.

Her desire to leave grew tenfold, though, when she saw who was standing behind that desk. She held in a groan as she recognized Anthony Pinker.

"Little Jeannie Lawson," the man said, sounding astonished. "I never thought I'd see you around after all this time."

Jeannette felt immediate distaste, even though nothing he'd said was particularly offensive. She still harbored a strong dislike for Anthony Pinker even after all these years.

When he was a senior and she was a sophomore, they had gone out for a few weeks. She had realized what kind of guy he was, childish and irresponsible, and the relationship had been short-lived. Still, it had been quite long enough to make her cringe now when she saw him again.

As if on cue, he smiled at her and leaned too far across the desk. "Maybe while you're in town we could go out sometime, catch up," he said in a low voice.

Jeannie could feel herself blushing from the embarrassment and annoyance. She couldn't believe she'd ever thought he was in any way attractive. Any words she meant to say flew out of her head and she froze there, staring at this man she had never expected to become a police officer, as he stood behind the desk in uniform.

Gustavo cleared his throat loudly from behind Jeannette and Anthony shifted his attention.

"Hi, sorry, you must be Jeannie's husband," Anthony said, suddenly polite.

Jeannette balked, her mind struggling to keep up with everything that was happening all at once. "No, no," she insisted, unsure why she felt so desperate to correct this awful man's misunderstanding. "This is Gustavo, my friend from school. He just moved back to town."

She saw the strain on Gustavo's face and knew that description bothered him, but had no idea what to do about that. She wished they could leave the police station and erase everything that had happened in the past two minutes, but she was pretty sure she'd never forget this level of embarrassment.

"Oh yes, Gustavo! Yeah, I remember you," Anthony said with a quick nod. He turned his attention to Jeannie. "How can I help you today?" he asked, giving her what she assumed was supposed to be a considerate expression that Jeannette didn't trust one bit.

Still, Jeannie was relieved to have a chance to change the conversation and turn it to the book and the mysterious thefts. She slid the book onto the counter in front of her. "Gustavo found this at the house he just bought, that old ranch over on Henley Street," she began.

Anthony grabbed it from the desk and absently

flipped through the pages. "I have no reports of missing copies of *A Christmas Carol*, so you can just keep it," he said with a smile.

Jeannette supposed he was trying to be funny, and she nearly stormed out right then and there, but she was determined to make him understand. She took a breath to calm the frustration building inside her. "No, Anthony, this is an important book. It's a counterfeit that was made when those books were stolen from the University of Kentucky. Do you remember that?"

Anthony's expression shifted for a moment, though she couldn't say what she saw in it, but then it went neutral. "And how do you know this book is connected to those thefts?"

That gave her pause. "Well, I don't know for *sure*, but I—"

"You don't know for sure," he repeated, cutting her off. "And those thefts happened almost two decades ago."

"Fifteen years ago," she corrected. "I've seen the replicas and—"

"Listen, Jeannie," he said, stopping her again, his voice serious, his frown deep. "Nothing is going to come of this. There are crimes we need to solve that are more important than digging into the disappearance of a few books years ago. And after all this time, even if we found the guilty person, we might not be able to get a conviction. Digging into the past won't help anyone at this point. It's time to forget about it," Anthony said, his voice firm.

Thoroughly upset, Jeannette turned around and Gustavo did the same.

As soon as the door shut behind them, Jeannette blew out a deep breath of frustration. "I should have made him listen to me. Or taken the book back. Now it's just going to sit in a box somewhere," she said, angry at herself.

"Hey," Gustavo said, putting a calming hand on her arm. "You did what you could do. That guy was a jerk, but he might be right about not being able to get a conviction."

Jeannette heard him, but she shook her head in disagreement. "We could still find those originals, get them back to where they belong. Even if we can't put the thief behind bars, that still matters."

She could see that he wanted to help, but he said nothing and she took a deep, calming breath. "It's fine," she said at last, though it didn't feel fine at all. "It's in the hands of the police, and if they choose not to do anything about it, that is outside of my control."

She tried to give Gustavo a look that said it was definitely not going to bother her forever that the case was going to go unsolved. His expression made it obvious he wasn't buying it one bit. "Or..." he said, "we could talk to Mr. Gibraltar."

"Who?" Jeannette asked, not recognizing the name.

"Mr. Gibraltar. He's the man who, up until a couple of months ago, lived in my house. For something like thirty years," he explained. "He's in a retirement home not too far from here."

Gustavo watched Jeannie's expression shift immediately to excitement. "You should know, he has dementia. I never spoke to him personally, but it seems like he doesn't always know where or when he is," he said.

He hated to burst her bubble, but he couldn't let her go into a meeting with him believing it would definitely be useful. She nodded, accepting this information, but her eyes still glittered. "If we *can* talk to him, though, he could know who made those books! Or he could have made them himself," she finished, clearly thinking through all the possibilities.

Gustavo shook his head. "I really don't think he would have. I know a bit of his story from his nieces, the ones who helped make the sale once his mind started to go, and also from the papers left around the place. His wife and son died a few years before the thefts happened and he's been running the ranch mostly on his own ever since. Not much in the way of education, but he was a hard worker and fair to everyone, from what people have told me."

Gustavo didn't say that he paid more for the ranch than he strictly needed to, and offered to clean out and fix up the place so Mr. Gibraltar's extended family wouldn't need to add that to their obligations, but he could tell by the look on Jeannie's face that she was guessing something along those lines.

"He could still have stolen those books," Jeannette told him. "You never know."

"If he did, I would very much like to hear that story," Gustavo said. "I don't see any harm in talking to him. If he knows anything and his mind is clear enough to talk about it, perhaps we could find those books. He's in a wheelchair and rather frail at this point, from what I've been told, but it's worth a shot."

"He lived on that ranch alone for all those years?" Jeannie asked, her voice sad.

Gustavo nodded. "That's what his niece said," he added.

"That must have been so lonely," she said.

Gustavo had thought the same thing, and he looked at Jeannie, wondering if she had been as lonely all these years as he'd been.

Jeannie was looking down, her expression one of empathy and perhaps some self-reflection, and it was difficult not to put a hand on her arm and show her that she wasn't alone.

"I'd like to see him, even if nothing comes of it," she said at last, coming out of her reverie.

Gustavo considered asking her about her life these past fifteen years—if she had missed him, too—but decided it was better to keep his thoughts on the task at hand.

He shifted his attention to his phone to find the

phone number for Mr. Gibraltar's retirement home. In short order, he was on the phone with the nurse, requesting a visit. She spoke for a minute and then hung up, and he turned back to Jeannie. She was standing beside him and staring off into the distance, lost in thought, and he wondered where her mind had gone. She saw that he was done and looked at him with hopeful eyes.

"He's having a bad day," he said, hating to disappoint her but unable to do anything about it. "They said to call tomorrow and see if he's doing better."

She was crestfallen for only a couple of moments, then perked up. "We could go to the library," she said.

He had expected her to ask to be taken home, so this came as a surprise. "The library at the university?" he asked.

She nodded. "They probably don't have the visitor logs from then, or they're in a box somewhere at that police station," she said, gesturing with her head toward the squat building. "But who knows what we might turn up."

Gustavo couldn't imagine they would turn up anything after so long, especially not anything the police hadn't seen, but he also didn't want to give up an opportunity to spend more time with Jeannie. Besides, it would be unkind to spoil her fun, and she knew much more about the library than he did, so he just gave her a smile and nodded. "I need to go back to my mom's and check on Angie before we drive out there," he told her. "It should only take a few minutes."

She didn't respond right away, looking uncomfortable. Finally she said, "Actually, if it's okay with you, I think I should talk to Linda about Mr. Gibraltar. If there's any useful information out there to know, she would probably be the one to know it. Gossiping with the town chatterboxes was always her favorite pastime."

He was curious if there was another reason she didn't want to go with him but decided not to pry. "Linda," he said, trying to place the name. "Oh yeah, that redheaded lady who owns that shop."

She raised her eyebrows at him. "The auburn-haired woman who has owned a curio shop in town for nearly thirty years," she corrected. He wasn't sure if she was being sassy or argumentative, but he couldn't help but smile.

Jeannie put a hand on her hip. "She's kept her finger on the pulse of Colby for decades and has a great memory. We've kept in touch and she's always up-to-date on what's happening. I doubt the internet will turn up much from that long ago, so someone like her could have some little piece of information that could lead us in the right direction. If Mr. Gibraltar had a renter or spent too much money in town, she would know about it."

Gustavo loved watching Jeannie in this type of mood: offended at being questioned and sure in her decision. When she was like this, he couldn't help but poke fun at least a little. "Wait, wait, wait. Aren't auburn and red the same?"

Jeannette gave him a face that said she didn't know whether to laugh or sigh. "That's the part that stuck out to you in all that, huh?" she asked, crossing her arms and giving him an exasperated look.

She was behaving like the high school version of herself with him, and he loved it. It was too easy—and felt too good—to joke and needle and laugh with her.

"Nope. I also heard that you're going to a shop where they might have some ornaments, which is fantastic because I could really use some more for my tree," he said, opening the truck door for her. "I can stop in for a minute and pick a few out before I leave you to enact your plan."

Jeannie smiled at his chivalry and climbed in. "A fact-finding and ornament-purchasing mission. Just like in the movies," she said when he'd walked around and settled in the driver's seat.

"Buckle up, Hutch," he said, turning on the vehicle.

"I'm definitely Starsky," Jeannie told him as she put on her seat belt.

Gustavo laughed in surprise, making her smile. "You're joking, right? Have you even *seen Starsky and Hutch*?"

Gustavo knew that she knew his fondness for old television shows and was reveling in his indignation.

"No, but I saw the movie trailer and I'm way more Ben Stiller than Owen Wilson," she told him.

The groan he gave was loud and pained, and it made her erupt into giggles. It was strange knowing someone so well despite not seeing them for a decade and a half, and it was clear she still knew him.

"Just keep an eye out for red—I mean *auburn* lights," he told her, making her giggle even harder. He started laughing, too. It felt so good to laugh with her. They drove and smiled, not saying much, and before he knew it, they had arrived downtown.

Jeannette calmed down enough to focus her attention on the main drag of her hometown, which sent a wave of nostalgia through her. The shop windows greeted her like old friends, sparkling with Christmas lights. It had been so many years and a few of the shops had changed, but overall it looked the same as it always had with its rows of stores attempting to entice those strolling along the sidewalks.

Jeannette thought of those hours she and Gustavo spent walking along those sidewalks hand in hand, talking and laughing the same way they had been just moments before. It was all so achingly beautiful that she felt tears prick her eyes. She'd forgotten how lovely her little town was, and suddenly she longed to be one of those weekend resident pedestrians rather than an outsider doing hardly more than passing through.

A couple walked along—the man pushing a stroller and the woman's arm wrapped around one of his—and Jeannette's lungs seemed unable to take in air.

She hadn't let herself think about what she was missing in her life as she holed up in a city she didn't enjoy—working herself to death in pursuit of the next step up the ladder—but here it was staring her right in the face and the knowledge was overwhelming. Especially with Gustavo sitting beside her, his eyes still sparkling with laughter.

Fortunately, Gustavo parked the car and she was able to put her mind back on the current task: finding out as much as she could about Mr. Gibraltar and anyone else who might have lived in that house when the theft happened. If they could find out where the book came from, she could solve the mystery and close this strange chapter in her life so she could get back to where she belonged. If she belonged anywhere.

She reminded herself that she was also excited to see her old friend, Linda. By avoiding this town so much since high school, she had also avoided the people she loved in that town.

People like her mother.

Her heart still ached for all those moments with her mom that she had missed by staying away. Her mother was a wonderful woman, and they had spoken on the phone frequently, but there had been too many moments she'd missed, and she would never get those chances back.

"You ready?" Gustavo asked, breaking into her thoughts.

# Chapter Four

Jeannette looked at Gustavo and considered telling him all these conflicting thoughts she was having—her desire to run away again and her desire to stay. Thoughts about her mom, who she hadn't let herself think about much these past couple of months. She could feel the grief just under the surface, waiting to break through. Gustavo had been a person she could tell almost everything to for so long, and the time she had kept secrets, she'd lost out on him and the life she had wanted.

But that time was over, and she had to remind herself of that. She could have a better relationship with people close to her and still live this life she had worked so hard for, and if she got too close to him, that might all slip away. Or she could get hurt again. And that thought was terrifying.

Jeannette took a calming breath. She pushed those feelings aside and started to open the door. Before she could see what he was doing, though, Gustavo had reached across her and grabbed it, stopping her. Leaned across her like that, he was closer to her than he'd been in fifteen years, and she resisted the urge to pull him into a tight hug. She could see his face in perfect detail, so familiar but older than she remembered. She wanted to press a hand to his cheek.

His eyes stared searchingly into hers. "I know you're dealing with a lot right now, Jeannie. If you ever want to talk about it, any of it, I'm here. I'm not going anywhere," he told her in a soft whisper that she felt to her toes.

*But I will be*, she thought, trying to keep the walls up to protect herself from the pain of getting too close and losing him again. She had no voice, so all she could do was nod and look away from him. He let go of the door and she pushed it all the way open, getting out of the car as quickly as she could. She needed room to breathe.

Gustavo got out, too, but he said nothing and didn't rush her. After a few moments, she was ready, and they walked along the sidewalk until they came to Linda's shop. Jeannette looked up at the sign, where a florid script read CuriosCity.

"I've never understood that name," Gustavo said musingly. "Why isn't there a space between them?"

Jeannette looked over at him, not sure if he was just trying to tease her for the whole Starsky and Hutch thing. This had to have come up at some point in their time together, hadn't it? "It's a play on words. You pronounce it like 'curiosity,'" she told him.

"Oh yeah, I get it now," he said, sounding a little embarrassed.

She chuckled at that and felt a little better for the moment. Then she turned her attention to the little shop.

How many hours had she spent there, looking through the bookshelves for special finds, chatting with Linda about whatever book she was reading, imagining what it would be like if she found something really valuable among the bric-a-brac?

That last one had always had a strong pull for her. She'd been so desperate to help her family live a little better, have nicer things...

She really couldn't blame Gustavo for suspecting she had a part in the thefts. It would have been entirely possible for her middle school musings to become high school actions, especially when she had access during her internship. If it had ever occurred to her to attempt it, she didn't know for sure if she would've been able to resist the temptation if the reward was big enough. She was embarrassed to admit that to herself, but it was true. She had hated being poor so much.

Gustavo opened the door to the shop and the little bell tinkled. Jeannette looked around, absorbing the familiar sights and sounds. Unlike some other parts of town, very little had changed in this shop, and she felt as if she was coming home after a very long time away. With Christmas season in full swing, the place was decorated in lights and garlands, holiday music played through speakers and several shoppers were wandering around looking for a unique gift some-one in their lives might treasure. She remembered it all so well, and how joyful it was to see a person's eyes light up when they found something perfect.

Linda stood at the counter, chatting with an el-derly woman Jeannette recognized as Mrs. Shelley, a common fixture at this store even all those years ago, back when Jeannette was a kid. Beside them stood a large tree covered in lights and dripping with ornaments.

"You confer with the auburn-haired owner of this establishment while I look through those ornaments," Gustavo whispered to Jeannette, as if they were part-ners in a heist.

Her lips twitched as she noticed that Linda's hair was still distinctly auburn, though the roots were de-cidedly gray. She nodded and together they walked through the shop, maneuvering to avoid jostling the crowded shelves.

When Jeannette was a few feet from the counter, Linda glanced up and spied her and the older woman's face split into a wide grin. "Little Jeannie! Oh wow, I never would have believed it!"

She was around the counter in a flash, and she squeezed Jeannette in a tight hug that was returned just as fervently. Jeannette had missed her old friend and was delighted to receive such a kind greeting.

Despite the age difference, the two women had been close for years, and Jeannette had a habit of coming in nearly every weekend for who knew how long, getting a bit paid here and there for stocking shelves and dusting while she and Linda chatted. Linda had been the one Jeannette had confided in, as a worried teenager, when she didn't know how to pay for university application fees or when she had a big exam coming up.

Or when her relationship started falling apart and she couldn't figure out why.

Jeannette blushed, regretting the amount of time that had passed since she'd last seen Linda. Quick yearly catch-up e-mails didn't do justice to their relationship all that time, and she was embarrassed to think about everything and everyone she had let herself forget about in her quest to leave behind any reminder of Gustavo and make as much money as possible.

But Linda behaved as if nothing had changed, giving Jeannette a glowing smile before her expression turned sad. "I heard about your mother, dear. I am so sorry. I used to sell her suncatchers here, as I'm sure you remember. I wish I still had some because they were always so beautiful. She was a rare woman, your mother," Linda told her.

Jeannette nodded, not trusting herself to speak.

Making suncatchers had been a hobby of her mother's, and she would sell them sometimes to help bring in a little cash, but it was something she'd done because she loved it and all the windows of the house had one or another that her mother had loved too much to sell. Jeannette was sure there were more hidden away, and thought maybe someday she'd see if her father would mind giving a few to people like Linda.

Not that she could imagine asking him that now, so soon. But maybe someday.

It was difficult for her to think about her mother when she had so nearly lost control of those emotions only a few minutes before. She wished she could talk to her mother about all the questions cropping up inside her, all the uncertainty. She knew Linda would be more than willing to listen to everything on her mind, but with Gustavo two feet away, filling his arms with ornaments, it would need to wait at least a few minutes.

For now, it was best to stick to other topics, and Jeannette cleared her throat and wiped away the single tear that had managed to escape.

Linda seemed interested in the topic of Gustavo, though, when she noticed him at the tree. "Gustavo Rodriguez, is that you?" she said, putting a hand on her hip and glancing from Jeannette to Gustavo with obvious interest.

Jeannette managed to avoid rolling her eyes at the

lack of subtlety. "He's just stopping in to grab a few ornaments for his tree."

Gustavo set an armful on the counter, the tree looking far barer than it had been moments before, and Linda walked behind the counter to ring them up and settle them carefully into a bag. "Angie is going to love this one," he told Jeannette, holding up a small porcelain angel. "I told her that her name has the word angel in it and now she's obsessed with them."

Jeannette's heart tugged at the image of the little girl excitedly adding the small angel to the tree, and it made her sad for a moment that she wasn't a part of that picture. Then Gustavo had his bag and turned to her. "You sure you don't want to come with me?"

Jeannette shook her head, sure he could see every emotion she was attempting to hide. "I'll stay here, thanks."

He paused for a moment, as if reconsidering. "Okay," he said at last. "I'll pick you up in about a half hour."

"You don't need to pick me up. I'm pretty heavy. If you drive over and come inside, I can just walk to the car and get in myself," she said, immediately regretting it when he gave her that playful grin she remembered.

It was too easy to fall into their old banter, and she reminded herself to avoid that from now on. Getting hurt would be too easy.

"Just drive over and walk inside. No picking up

required. Got it," he said as if he was carefully noting this new plan.

She tried to hide her grin, and his eyes looked into hers for another few moments before he turned away and left the little shop.

Jeannette turned to see Linda and Mrs. Shelley watching her carefully, and she had the urge to get away from those probing eyes for a few minutes. "Where is Henry?" she asked, looking around the store for his mop of copper curls.

Henry was always around his mother's shop somewhere, stacking shelves carefully, dusting or examining some object he found intriguing. He always seemed happiest when he had something to do.

"He's straightening the pill boxes right now. He just loves organizing those," Linda told her, pointing toward a nearby aisle.

Jeannette would talk to Linda about the book Gustavo had found and Mr. Gibraltar, but the only thing Linda would want to discuss was Gustavo, and Jeannette knew she wasn't ready for that. So first she would say hi to Henry. "I'll be back in a couple of minutes," she told Linda.

Then she quickly greeted Mrs. Shelley and went off in search of Henry and the pill boxes, taking a deep breath once she was away from all the watchful eyes. As soon as she walked into the aisle, she spotted the large man and his signature curls, though they had darkened and there was a smattering of white hairs mixed in, even though he wasn't much more than forty. He was moving the tiny objects with the most delicate movements.

He looked so intent on his task that she ultimately decided not to bother him when he looked up. "Jean-Jean!" he shouted, much too loud in the quiet store, and he ran over to give her a big hug. "You were gone a long time!" he told her.

Jeannette almost burst into tears. She *had* been gone a long time, and no matter how many times she'd thought about Henry and his mom, she had been so busy with her own life and avoiding Gustavo that she hadn't dropped in just to say hello. She resolved to be a better friend. "I'm sorry I was gone so long," she told him. "I will see you more. I promise."

His eyes lit up. "Will you visit tomorrow?" he asked.

Jeannette laughed at his enthusiasm. "Yes, I'll come by tomorrow. You can show me all the new things and tell me about what has happened since I was here last."

Henry seemed nearly giddy at the idea and spent several minutes describing the activities of the past week, with Jeannette listening intently. Before he could start describing each lunch, however, she stopped him, aware that time was slipping by and she had come to visit for a very particular reason. "I can't wait to hear more tomorrow, Henry, but right now I need to talk to your mom. Do you want to come with me?"

Henry shook his head. "I'm making the little boxes look nice," he said very seriously.

Jeannette gave him one more hug and then headed toward the register, her heart feeling full in a way it hadn't in a long time. Henry was the kind of person who always made you feel like that. He was the sweetest, most genuinely loving person she had ever met, and she couldn't wait to come back tomorrow and watch his face light up again.

Linda and Mrs. Shelley were still standing together and talking, and Jeannette had no doubt the two of them were discussing the former high school sweethearts who had walked into the store together only a few minutes ago. When Jeannette reached the register, Linda smiled at her and leaned on the counter. "Sounds like Henry was as happy to see you as I am," Linda told her.

Jeannette laughed. "He is as wonderful as ever. I promised him I'd stop by tomorrow."

"Oh that's so nice of you. He loves visits from friends," Linda said, looking fondly in the direction where Henry was, even though she couldn't see him.

Linda adored her son with a fervor that was almost overwhelming to experience. She had taken care of him all these years, since she was a young single mother, without a word of complaint. He was her pride and joy, and you could see it in every line of her face.

"So what brings you here today, Jeannie?" Linda asked. Her glance darted toward the Christmas tree Gustavo had so recently pillaged, and she raised her eyebrows with a silent question Jeannette didn't really know how to answer.

"Gustavo and I are trying to solve a mystery," Jeannette explained, trying to intrigue the older women enough to distract them from their interest in her love life. "And I thought you might know some old town goings-on that could help us solve it."

Mrs. Shelley broke into the conversation. "Trying to solve a mystery, little Jeannie!"

Jeannette nodded and had to listen to a long tale about the mysterious disappearance of her toy poodle. Finally, her story ended when they found the poor thing stuck in a cardboard box it was too little to jump out of. "Heaven only knows how she got in there in the first place," Mrs. Shelley added with a laugh.

Jeannette nodded politely and agreed that it was very fortunate the little thing was found, and only then was she able to turn to Linda, who was leaning forward now that Mrs. Shelley's story was over. "What's this mystery?" she asked Jeannette. Mrs. Shelley leaned in, too, ready to listen.

Jeannette smiled, knowing exactly how much her friend was going to enjoy this. "We found a book over at Mr. Gibraltar's old ranch and we think it has something to do with a theft from the university library fifteen years ago. Do you know anything about Mr. Gibraltar or anyone that might have been living with him? This was shortly after his wife died. If anybody stayed with him at that time, or if you have any other interesting information about the man or the fake books, we might discover who stole the originals."

Linda blinked. "Fifteen years ago?" she asked incredulously, knitting her brows.

"I know it's a long time, and I don't expect you to remember much," Jeannette assured her. "It was just a random hope that you might recall something."

Linda thought carefully, silent for long moments. "I think Mr. Gibraltar might have taken in people around that time to help pay the mortgage, but I can't imagine where you would find information about that. I'm sure he would just do handshake deals. He was a rancher, not a businessman."

Jeannette sighed. No records meant no leads. "I don't suppose you know the names of anyone who stayed there around that time?" she asked, knowing it was a long shot.

Linda squinted into the distance, and then her eyes lit up. "Actually, I think there was a young man who lived there for a while, right around that time. His name was John, maybe," Linda said, looking triumphant. "I imagine he could've been one to do such a thing. Didn't like his character."

Jeannette absorbed this information. It wasn't much, but it was something. It might be possible to track down that man somehow.

"Have you discussed your discovery with the police?"

Jeannette nodded, her thoughts shifting from this John person to her experience at the police station. "They weren't very helpful. Said we probably couldn't get a conviction."

*Though I doubt Anthony would have cared even if that wasn't true*, she thought.

It might not be something exciting like a murder, but she wanted to solve this case and find those stolen books. Not just because she wanted to get the books returned, but also because she hadn't had something this interesting to think about for years. And with the knowledge that this theft had played its own part in the loss of her first love, it felt important that she solve it.

"Perhaps that information will help them," Linda said. "You should mention it if you talk to them again."

"Well," chimed in Mrs. Shelley, taking on the voice of someone about to dispense hard-earned wisdom. "It's exciting to think about—figuring out some old case, you know—but that is what the police are for, after all, and if they say it's time to let it lie, then this isn't something for a sweet thing like you to worry yourself over. Officers understand crime and criminals in a way we simply don't, and you never know what meddling could do. We can't all—"

Jeannette's phone dinged and she shifted her attention to it, grateful for the distraction from what seemed to be a rather long lecture.

It was Gustavo, saying he would be there in just a few minutes to pick her up, er, get her. Jeannette was surprised to see that the time had passed by so quickly.

"I need to leave soon," she told Linda, "Is there anything else you could tell me about Mr. Gibraltar or anything?"

Linda shook her head slowly. "I don't believe I ever actually met the man myself, dear. I'm sorry."

Jeannette sighed, a little disappointed. Still, there was the possibility of that renter, and that could be something.

"I worry about you getting caught up in a crime, Jeannette, even an old one," Mrs. Shelley said, her voice serious. "I've heard many stories of cold cases, and sometimes investigating can lead to danger."

Jeannette nodded and thanked her, then said her goodbyes and promised to visit the next day before rushing out to where Gustavo waited. She was excited to tell him about the new, though small, developments.

When she hopped in the car, Gustavo looked delighted to see her, and she smiled back. Intellectually she knew that he could have been with his wife, but emotionally she couldn't help but see him as the same boy she had fallen in love with all those years ago.

"Are you ready to see a library?" he asked her.

She looked incredulous. "I think you know what a silly question that is," she told him, and he started the truck.

She was practically bouncing in her seat on the drive. Even if they found out nothing about the theft, she was going to the University of Kentucky's rare books library, and she loved that place like a second home. It was a place of peace and calm, where nothing mattered but the beauty of the written word.

"Did you find out anything interesting?" Gustavo asked as they pulled onto the road toward Lexington.

"Actually, there was something. Linda thought a man named John rented a room from Mr. Gibraltar around that time."

"John, huh? That's not much to go on," he responded. The town wasn't that big, but there had to be quite a few Johns around, and still more that could have been passing through fifteen years ago.

"I know, but it's something. Maybe if we can see the old visitor records at the library, a name will pop out at us."

He nodded and the conversation died. Gustavo let the silence last for a few minutes before deciding to bring up the topic he'd been avoiding since the police station. She'd been too flustered and frustrated then, but his brain kept circling back to that conversation and he couldn't seem to let it go. "That was a pretty awkward interaction with Anthony," he prompted, glancing at her out of the side of his eye.

It took her a moment to absorb what he had said before giving a little snort. "That man is just as childish as he was in high school," she said with a little shake of her head.

"But you went out with him in high school," he said.

She flushed and he almost felt bad for bringing it up, but it was true. He had watched that smarmy guy smile at Jeannie and Jeannie smile back, and it had driven him crazy. He was deeply in love with his good friend Jeannette by that time, and every time he saw her with Anthony he'd wanted to do something, anything, to get her away from him.

Fortunately, it had only lasted a couple of weeks or he might have tried to fight Anthony, which probably wouldn't have turned out well for Gustavo, the skinny little sophomore. Now, though—

"I still can't believe I dated him," she said with a shudder. "There was a very brief time when I thought he might actually be a decent person and, well…" she said, drifting off.

"Well, what?" he asked, genuinely curious what

could have possibly made her think it was a good idea to date Anthony.

"Well," she said again, blushing up to her ears, "I hoped dating him would help me get over you."

He looked at her, shocked. "But you didn't like me then," he told her.

Jeannie rolled her eyes at him. "I was crazy about you since eighth grade, Gustavo. After more than a year of dropping hints, I figured you'd never like me that way and I tried dating. Obviously, that didn't go well. You fell for me junior year, but I'd been completely in love with you for such a long time by that time. I can't believe you never knew."

"You liked me in eighth grade?" he asked, trying to rewrite the entire story of their friendship. "I was in love with you since seventh."

"Oh come on, it isn't a competition," Jeannie said.

Gustavo couldn't believe how ridiculous they had been. "We had been just friends for years, but I fell in love with you during Mrs. Cranston's class. There was something about the way you tapped your pencil on your desk as you tried to figure out Algebra that made me into a puddle of goo."

"Well then, you certainly should have asked me out before I went out with Anthony," she said, making him laugh.

"You're right. Next time. I promise."

The air in the vehicle seemed to shift in a moment,

suddenly feeling too warm and heavy, and the laughter stopped.

He rolled down the window and took a deep breath, wondering what she would say if he asked her out now.

Neither of them said anything for the rest of the drive.

Jeannette watched the scenery out the window as they drove, unsure what to say to the person she'd loved for so much of her childhood and avoided nearly her entire adulthood. It was a strange situation to be in.

She also couldn't believe how things had changed over the years. She had driven through these same areas so many times, going to the city for various reasons, then to the library practically every week of her high school years. She'd gone there to complete her community service hours, drawn to the biggest library in the area, and when they offered her an opportunity at a minimum wage job doing basic shelving and some bookkeeping, she'd jumped at the chance.

Gustavo parked in the guest lot and they walked toward the large stone building, looking as important as a church, holding within it the wisdom and imagination of more people than she could count, all waiting to share their knowledge.

Jeannette savored each step. The experience at the police station had been frustrating, but she knew this would ease her tension even if she and Gustavo learned nothing about the theft. It was like visiting an old friend, and she was sorry she'd been away so long.

As they approached the entrance, Gustavo stepped forward and opened the door for her, making her blush a little. He had always been a thoughtful boy, and it seemed he hadn't changed much in the intervening years.

They walked through the large building toward the service desk, Jeannette glancing around. In here, hardly anything had changed, and that made her smile. When she saw who was standing behind the service desk, that smile widened into a huge grin. "Hi, Brayden," she said as she approached.

Brayden looked at her with that searching look of someone who couldn't put a name to a face, and Jeannette felt a pang yet again for having stayed away from everyone so long. "Jeannie Lawson," she told him.

His eyes lit up. "Jeannie! It's been, what, a decade since you worked here?" he said, coming around the desk to hug her.

"Longer," she said with a laugh as he squeezed her tight. Brayden was a big bear of a man, but was as friendly and kind as a person could be.

She noticed his hair had more gray in it than it used to, and he had settled firmly into middle age, but he seemed as gentle and kind as ever. "Did you come by just to catch up, or is there something I can do for you?"

She felt a thrill of excitement, knowing her audience here would be much more receptive than Anthony at the police station had been. "You remember the books that were stolen fifteen years ago? And replaced with fakes?"

Brayden raised his eyebrows. "Of course I do. I'm still embarrassed we had no idea. Why? Did something new happen in the case?"

Jeannette could hardly contain her excitement. "Gustavo," she said, pointing at him, "found another replica in the house he just bought."

Brayden looked at Gustavo, and Jeannette imagined it was similar to how she looked when she realized what he'd brought her. Brayden's mouth hung open, his eyes wide. "You *found* one! How did you know?" he asked, his words coming out in an excited rush.

Gustavo shook his head. "I had no idea. It was all Jeannie," he said.

Brayden's gaze switched back to Jeannette, and she could feel herself blushing. "We had talked about those fakes for hours back then, remember? It was just like them."

Brayden beamed at her with pride. "I'm impressed," he said. "So, show me!"

Jeannette grimaced. "We gave it to the police,

thinking it might help them finally catch the thieves, but it seems like they're not going to do much about it."

"So why are you here? Do I get to help solve the mystery of the missing tomes?" Brayden said, making it sound like the title of a *Nancy Drew* novel.

Jeannette laughed. "Actually, maybe. Is there any chance the library kept those logs that showed who entered the rare books section?" she asked.

She expected Brayden to look disappointed, but instead he nodded enthusiastically. "In the storage room. There are at least thirty years of records."

Jeannette felt excitement bubbling up. "Do you know if the police took the ones from that year?" she asked.

Brayden shrugged. "I have no idea, but we can go check," he said. He turned to a young woman who was stacking books a few feet away. "I'll be back in a few minutes, Holly."

The woman nodded and took his place at the desk and off he went, nearly bouncing his way through the stacks, with Jeannette and Gustavo following him and sharing a little grin as they went.

Jeannette couldn't believe how strange a turn her day had taken. She'd woken up with a plan to run a few errands and spend the afternoon helping her sister around the house, and now here she was visiting so many Ghosts of Christmases Past and trying to find clues to a long-unsolved crime with her old boyfriend. It was all so unexpected that it made her head spin.

They followed Brayden down a hallway and he pulled out his keys, unlocked one of the doors and held it open, ushering Jeannette and Gustavo inside. The room was large and obviously little-used, with cardboard boxes stacked onto shelves and a very old computer tucked in the corner. Jeannette had been in there a few times when she worked for the library, and it looked essentially the same. Just a place to keep stuff that wasn't useful but wasn't supposed to be thrown away for one reason or another.

Brayden showed them to the corner where one shelf held three-ring binders, many of them yellowed with age. They each had a year written on the side, and Brayden gestured with a flourish. "There you are, the logs for the rare books library," he told them.

Jeannette wondered if it would really be so simple, but then realized she didn't really know what she was expecting to find out from these old logs. She looked at Gustavo and he clearly was thinking the same thing. "I suppose we just look and see if Mr. Gibraltar's name is on there? Or the name Linda mentioned?" he asked.

She shrugged and pulled out the binder she wanted. "She said she was pretty sure his name was John. That's not much to go on," she told him.

Gustavo shrugged. "So we write down every John we find and do some research, see where that gets us," he said.

That sounded like a wild-goose chase, but she had

no better ideas, so she opened the binder and looked over the page of scribbled names, hoping something would pop out at her.

"Do you think the thief would actually use their real name?" Gustavo asked in a quiet whisper. "Why not just use a fake one?"

"People need to show ID to get into the rare books section," Brayden said from behind them, glancing at the list with interest. "So their real name will be on there, unless they had a fake ID, too. That would be so interesting!"

Jeannette was less excited about that possibility than Brayden was. She started looking through, trying to decipher various handwritings and pointing out each John they found so Gustavo snapped a photo of them with his phone.

Ten minutes later, they had several names, but Jeannette felt no closer to solving the theft. There were a few names that repeated, and they noted those, too, but nothing much felt familiar or significant. She returned the binder to the shelf, trying not to look too disappointed.

"Thanks, Brayden. I really appreciate you helping us out and I'll let you know if we solve it."

"You better," he told her. "I expect to hear all about how you cracked the case. And if you ever want a job here, you know I've got you covered," he added.

Jeannette's heart tugged at those words. She would love to work at the library again, but knew she would never make enough there to live comfortably, even in Kentucky. "Thank you, Brayden," she said, and she meant it.

He gave her a last hug, then walked them outside and gave her and Gustavo a little wave as they left.

The afternoon had turned chilly, and Jeannette pulled her coat around herself as they walked toward the car, each thinking their own thoughts.

"You hungry?" Gustavo asked, realizing they had both skipped lunch and it was nearly dinner time.

Jeannie looked surprised for a moment, and Gustavo suppressed a smile. He remembered all too well how often Jeannie would forget to eat when she was caught up in her own thoughts. Food just didn't occur to her sometimes. "I'm starving," she admitted.

He nodded and turned off the road, and in a few minutes they were sitting in a small diner, waiting for hamburgers. Gustavo watched Jeannie as she drew small circles with her finger on the table, lost in thought.

"Well, that wasn't very helpful," she said at last, looking despondent.

Gustavo leaned toward her, his expression serious. "Maybe we shouldn't keep digging into this," he suggested gently. "It doesn't seem to be going anywhere, and this is probably something best left to the police."

She raised her eyebrows, as if that idea was ludicrous. "The police don't care," she reminded him.

"And I need to know what happened. We haven't even talked to Mr. Gibraltar yet. I can work on it by myself if you like, but we've hardly tried at all and I'm not ready to call it quits."

She leaned back against the booth cushion and crossed her arms. Gustavo could see she was absolutely determined, but he had to wonder if they really knew what they were getting into with this, and he had a gut feeling that they didn't. After all, somebody had committed a crime, and he wondered if maybe Jeannie had forgotten about that aspect in her determination to get answers.

Still, he wasn't going to let her carry on by herself, and even if she wanted to stop now, could they just dismiss this whole thing and get back to their normal lives without ever finding out why that book ended up at his place? He doubted it.

"If you're in, I'm in. We should look around my house more," he told her, hoping for a reconciliation. "See if there's anything else there that might tell us more about who made those books."

Jeannie didn't answer right away, and he watched her, wondering what thoughts were tumbling through that head of hers. She was staring down at the table, biting her lip. She looked nervous.

"Something wrong?" he asked, surprised at her reaction.

"No, I want to search for more information. I'm just worried I'll be in the way," she said.

"In the way?" he asked, confused. "My mom will bring Angie over at some point and I'll need to put her down for bed, and that's always a nightmare, but other than that we can search to your heart's content."

She still seemed nervous, though he wasn't sure why. "Do you want me to take you home instead?" he asked.

She was silent for a moment before finally shaking her head. "No, I'd like to see if there is anything there to help us," she said at last.

Gustavo kept his eyes on her as their food arrived. Jeannie looked relaxed as she smiled and thanked the server, but he could tell she was uncomfortable. Why would she feel like she might be in the way? It was just him and Angie, and—

*Oh.*

"Angie and I live at the ranch alone," he said as soon as the server left. "Her mom isn't in the picture."

By the expression on Jeannie's face, he knew he'd hit the nail on the head. The fry she had picked up was frozen in midair.

He couldn't believe that he hadn't once mentioned this in all these hours. He'd been so focused on his feelings and the mystery at hand that he hadn't even thought about what Jeannie might have concluded when he walked up with a daughter in tow.

"She basically left Angie on my doorstep a few months ago. Just showed up one day, told me the girl was my responsibility, signed over her custody to me and left. It was the first time I knew I even had a daughter," he explained.

"So you're single," she said, relief clear in her voice. "I mean..." she drifted off and blushed, shoving the fry into her mouth and looking away from him, which made him smile.

He wondered why it had taken him so long to figure out what Jeannie was worried about. Maybe it was because Angie's mom was so far from his mind, or maybe it hadn't occurred to him that Jeannie might have feelings about him with a partner.

"Yep, single," he said, picking up his burger. He was embarrassed to say the rest so he chewed his first bite slowly and thought about how to tell her about his life since he'd seen her last. Finally, he continued. "I went through some ugly times when I was living in Chicago, working as a lawyer. I was so unhappy there, I did everything I could not to feel much of anything for a long time. A lot of things I'm not very proud of. And then suddenly I found out I had this amazing little girl and it's absolutely terrifying," he said, speaking fast, confiding in the one person he'd ever really trusted. "I have no idea what I'm doing and I fail at it every day, but my life finally has meaning and I thank God for Angie every single day and I just hope I can give her the life she deserves."

They ate in silence for a few minutes. Gustavo wondered if Jeannie would see him differently now. He wouldn't blame her.

After another French fry, she looked at him, and he saw only compassion and understanding in her eyes. "Do you think her mother will ever come back into the picture?" she asked.

Gustave gave a sad little smile. "She wasn't a good mother to Angie and she knew it. She signed away her parental rights, took a chunk of money and left. Maybe someday she'll want to be in Angie's life again and I hope she will, but I'm the girl's only parent in the eyes of the law."

Jeannie didn't respond, and Gustavo felt as if he needed to change the subject, move to topics that didn't remind him of the poor choices he'd made in his life. "That was nice of Brayden to offer you a job," he said, grasping for something.

Jeannie let out a little laugh. "Yeah, if I was willing to move to Kentucky and work for almost nothing, it would be perfect," she said with a shake of her head.

"What do you do now?" he asked, curious.

"I'm in advertisement," she said, and he saw the way her lips pinched together, as if the thought was unpleasant.

"You make ads?" he asked, trying to sound interested rather than simply surprised. He had never expected that to be her job, just assuming it would be something to do with writing. That had always been her passion.

She shrugged. "I manage people who make ads," she clarified. "But I tweak them here and there to make them more effective before they get sent to the companies."

The monotone way she explained her job wasn't what he expected from somebody as passionate as Jeannie. He would have thought she would gush over her work, sharing details about it with that spark of excitement he loved so much about her.

"Do you enjoy it?" he asked, even though he was sure he knew the answer.

She didn't answer right away, keeping her eyes on the nearly empty plate in front of her. "It's good money," she said at last. "And if I keep working hard, I'll be up for a big promotion soon and then I'll have a lot more freedom."

*Ah, the money thing*, Gustavo thought. He wanted to help Jeannie see that there were so many things more important than money.

# Chapter Five

Jeannette tried to process all she'd learned about Gustavo as they settled back into the truck for the drive back to Colby. It was so much to absorb. There wasn't a wife hidden away somewhere, living the life Jeannette had dreamed about for more years than she cared to admit. And that poor little girl, to be dropped that way. She thanked God that Angie had fallen into Gustavo's loving hands, where she would be safe and well cared for.

She watched him out of the corner of her eye while he drove, and she wondered what kind of life they could have had. They could have…

But no. She couldn't do that after how hard she'd worked, could she? He obviously hated being a lawyer and was content to scratch out a living on a ranch in their hometown. As much as she loved Colby, would she be willing to give up everything she'd worked for to live a life like her parents, always watching the bank account at the end of the month and hoping there would be enough to get by?

The idea terrified her.

In what felt like no time, they were at Mr. Gibraltar's old house—the place that now belonged to Gustavo. It looked a bit rundown, but she could see why Gustavo had bought it. Homey, with lots of land, it was exactly the place he had talked about owning someday. She looked over and saw the hope in his eyes as they pulled up to his home, and she needed to remind herself that this was not what she wanted. She took a breath and shifted her attention to the sky, heavy with rain clouds.

"We have a bit of time before my mom gets here with Angie. How about we take a look around now, while it's calm?" he asked, turning toward her.

Jeannette suddenly felt shy, as if there was some kind of impropriety in her and Gustavo being alone in his house together. That he might get the wrong impression about what they're relationship was or could be. But she swallowed that and nodded. They were investigating, after all, not romancing.

"The house is a bit of a mess," he confessed. "I just moved in and the furniture isn't even here yet, and—"

"It's fine," she reassured him. "I'm looking for clues, not the winning submission to *Lovely Living Rooms Magazine*. Besides, it's just me," she said, giving him a little smile.

The look he gave her sent a shiver through her—

she could practically hear him thinking that she was more than *just* her—and old feelings unfurled inside her. Flustered, she turned away from him and opened the door of the truck, hearing him do the same. They started walking toward the house, Jeannette's thoughts a jumble. She reminded herself to stay focused on why she was there.

"I want to see where Angie found that book and look for any other little odds and ends. Something unexpected could be important. And you said the sellers didn't clean out the place before they left. If there are any financial documents, those might give us some clues. Can you show me his old papers?" Jeannette asked as they stepped onto the porch.

"I *can*," Gustavo responded with a mischievous grin, not moving from where he stood beside the front door.

Jeannie rolled her eyes in mock exasperation. "Oh no, Gustavo, I can't believe you're still doing that! Fine. *Will* you show me?" she asked, using the grammatically correct form and trying unsuccessfully to hide a smile.

He laughed quietly and unlocked the door. "I've only ever done that to you, you know," he told her as she followed. "You're the smartest person I know and it's funny that you don't remember that one rule. I can't help myself."

"You *can*," she replied sarcastically, using his words against him.

His laughter boomed unexpectedly loud in the

silence, and it made Jeannette grin. She'd always loved his laugh. It was so genuine, so full of honest joy. He'd been a pretty serious kid, not very happy at home, but when she managed to make him laugh, his true self shone through, and she had lived for those moments.

Jeannette felt a deep longing she hadn't experienced for a very long time, and it worried her.

It was true she had missed Gustavo—more than she could possibly say. But would she be willing to give up her job and her promotion and everything she had worked for in the last fifteen years to live on this ranch? It was a wonderful place and she could see being happy there, but the pain from her childhood was still there, digging into her with its claws. She had hated being poor so much as a kid, and willingly throwing herself into a similar life as an adult was terrifying, even if it was to be with a person she loved.

And she did love him. In fact, she had never stopped loving him.

But would love be enough to make her happy?

She was still wondering this as she stepped inside Gustavo's house. As soon as she was in the door, though, all her thoughts stuttered to a halt as she stared at Gustavo, worried by the expression on his face. He was looking around as though he was lost, but he was in his own home. She couldn't understand it.

"Someone's been here," he said, sounding confused.

She looked around and immediately saw what he meant. Though the place had very little in it, the living room looked as if someone had come in and thrown around anything they could reach. Two large bookshelves were knocked over, and tools were scattered across the room. A Christmas tree lay on its side, the few ornaments on the ground. Some of them were broken.

She managed to tear her eyes from the heartbreaking sight and looked through a doorway into a small bedroom, and it was the same thing there. A chair had been turned over and children's books littered the floor.

Jeannette couldn't believe it, and based on Gustavo's frozen look, neither could he. Her first thought was that it was good Gustavo had so few things because it wouldn't be too much work to clean it up, though the ornaments would need to be replaced. Her second thought was that someone must have done this, and that person could still be in the house, waiting. What if they were in danger?

"Gustavo, we need to get out of here," Jeannette said in a whisper, pulling at his arm. She felt as if she was being watched and glanced around, her fingers tingling with the adrenaline pumping through her body as panic set in.

When Gustavo didn't move, Jeannette knew she

needed to be the voice of reason in this moment; she had to get them to safety.

"Gustavo," she said emphatically, gripping his arm tight. He finally turned to look at her, his eyes taking a moment to focus on her. "We need to get out of here right now," she told him, her words slow and clear to get through the fog in his brain. "Someone could still be here. It might not be safe."

That seemed to be what Gustavo needed to hear. He jerked, looking more awake than he had a few moments before, and suddenly began to move again. He quickly ushered her out the door, and Jeannette moved toward the truck at a near-run, feeling the reassuring pressure of Gustavo's hand on her back.

They hauled themselves into the truck and Jeannette buckled her seat belt, her eyes scanning the house and everything she could see, looking for danger.

"I don't know where to go," Gustavo told her as he put the keys in the ignition.

Jeannie's mind was whirring in overdrive. "We need to make sure your mom and Angie are safe and don't come here," she said. "Let's go there. You should call to let them know, and call the police, too. How about I drive so you can do that?"

He nodded and she climbed over him, unwilling to get out of the truck in order to switch places. Before she started the truck, though, she pulled her phone from her pocket and sent a quick text to her father and sister. She wouldn't breathe properly unless she knew they were okay.

A few seconds later, they were on the road toward Gustavo's childhood home, and Gustavo's phone was plastered to his ear. Jeannette could feel her pulse rushing in her ears, and her mind was jumping between what had happened and the silent phone in her lap, but she didn't take her eyes off the road.

She listened to Gustavo make a brief call to his mother and then the police, but she couldn't concentrate on the words he was saying to them. Her mind was repeating the same thoughts over and over, like a broken record.

Someone had broken into Gustavo's house and tossed things around. Why? She tried to tell herself that it had nothing to do with the book, that it was just coincidence. And that was possible, but deep down she didn't believe it.

But why would somebody care if they looked into the theft? Jeannette didn't know enough about the law, but was whatever trouble the person might get into enough to make them commit new crimes now? And how did they even know?

Maybe it wasn't just the book theft whoever-it-was was worried about. Perhaps if she and Gustavo kept digging, they would discover there was more here than a few missing rare books. Something big. Something worth breaking into Gustavo's house for.

Would it be worth enough to commit other crimes? Violent ones?

Jeannette pulled her mind back to the present, realizing she was letting her thoughts spin out of control.

Soon she pulled up to the tall white house, the lights in the window bright and welcoming, and she heard Gustavo tell the person on the phone with him that he would call again, hanging up abruptly. She doubted the police would like that much, but it was obvious Gustavo had another priority.

As soon she stopped the truck, he rushed out of the vehicle and up to the door, clearly anxious to see his daughter. At that moment, Jeannette's phone dinged and she grabbed it like a drowning person grasping for a life preserver. It was her father, saying everyone was fine and asking if something was wrong.

The relief was almost overwhelming, and she sent back some message, though she wasn't entirely sure it was coherent. Once that was complete, she leaned back in the driver's seat of the truck, alone now that Gustavo had run inside. Her family was safe.

She understood that she could get out of the vehicle and walk into the house, but Jeannette didn't move. Now that they were somewhere away, and everyone was safe, all the panic and fear she had tamped down began to rush through her, immobilizing her in the seat. She leaned her head against the steering wheel, her breath hitching in her throat as her body released all the emotion she hadn't let herself feel.

After a minute or two, the driver's door opened and Jeannette turned her head to see Gustavo there, holding Angie in his arms. "Hey, Jeannie, you okay?" he asked, his voice soft and calm.

Jeannette didn't know how to answer that. It seemed Gustavo didn't need an answer, though, and he held out his hand to her. "Come inside," he said, and she took his hand, feeling hers shaking and his steady and warm.

Inside the house, Gustavo's mother greeted Jeannette with a hug, and it was so different from the stern welcomes she'd received in childhood that the strangeness of it broke through Jeannette's anxiety a little. Even the house seemed softer—less cold—and children's toys littered the floor.

"That must have been so frightening, dear," the older woman said, shaking her head. "Who would do such a thing?"

Gustavo and Jeannette exchanged a glance, and it was clear he was thinking along the same lines she was: somebody who didn't want them to find out more about a crime.

Jeannette reminded herself that she was jumping to a conclusion and sometimes break-ins just happen. "I should go home," she said.

She didn't want to leave Gustavo and his calming presence, but she knew she wouldn't be able to breathe properly until she'd seen her family and made sure everyone was safe. Gustavo seemed to understand. "Give me five minutes to get Angie to bed and then I'll take you. Angie, we're going to have a sleepover with Beba," he said, smiling at the little girl in an attempt to make the change of plans sound like a treat.

"No, Papa! Not sleepy!" Angie wailed, as if on cue, her body going limp in his arms.

Jeannette felt for the man as he sighed. "I'm sorry," he told Jeannette as he hauled the wailing girl up the stairs.

Jeannette could hear the cries of "Not sleepy!" getting fainter and fainter, finally muffled by a closed door, and Gustavo's mother sighed. "That poor girl does this every night. It must be so difficult for Gustavo. I blame that mother of hers leaving her like that," she said, showing some of that old terseness Jeannette had always associated with the woman. "Angie doesn't believe her father will be there for her tomorrow, but he will. He is a good man, Gustavo," she finished.

Jeannette watched the stairs, wishing there was something she could do to help.

Gustavo stood outside the door, rubbing his temples and praying that he wouldn't start a tantrum of his own if Angie screamed again. Every night had been like this since her mother had brought the girl to his apartment, and he was doing his best but felt like he was failing her every single time.

He waited, listening for more shouting, but after a couple of minutes, it seemed like the danger had passed, and he tiptoed downstairs, where Jeannie and his mother waited.

"I'll be back soon," he said to his mother as he put on his shoes. "If she starts to shout—"

The older woman waved a hand. "I have been wanting Angie to stay since I learned I had a grand-daughter. It will be fine. Drive safe," she told him.

Gustavo nodded and kissed her on the cheek before turning to Jeannie and walking with her out the door. The truth was, he didn't want to take her home, even if he knew she would be safe with her father and sister. He would worry every moment she was out of his sight, but what could he do?

So he and Jeannie made their way out to the truck, looking everywhere for dangers that might be lurking in the dark as they went. The only sound was wind in the trees, but he couldn't stop wondering if someone was out there, watching them.

Gustavo tried to seem calm, though, for Jeannie's sake. He could see how shaken she was, and the look she'd had on her face when he helped her out of the truck a few minutes before had been so frightened and lost that it made his heart ache. She'd been strong when it counted, but he knew she needed to crumble under the weight of the worry she had experienced in that moment, and he would be steady while she did so.

He led her to the passenger side and opened the door for her. She climbed in silently and he closed her door firmly before walking to the driver's side.

They drove silently toward her father's home, the familiar roads feeling almost sinister in the dark.

Gustavo glanced over at Jeannie, who was staring out the window and rubbing her lip—the same thing she'd done when she was worrying even as a girl. He wanted to comfort her somehow, but didn't know exactly how to do that. He felt so close to her in some ways, but there was still a distance between them he didn't know how to bridge.

"Angie is very blessed to have you," Jeannie told him suddenly, surprising him out of his reverie.

He gave her a grateful smile. "I'm trying to make this a happy life for her," he said.

"The break-in might not help with that," she said, half laughing, half sobbing.

He pulled the truck to the side of the road and turned to her. "Hey, it's okay," he reassured her, putting a hand on her shoulder. "Angie is safe. We're all safe," he said, hoping he was telling the truth.

Jeannie nodded, though she still looked close to tears, and he leaned across and hugged her. She clasped him tightly, and he could feel her heart pounding, her breath fast. His arms remembered this feeling as if no time had passed. He stroked her hair and held her until she calmed a little and finally broke away.

"I'm sorry," she said, wiping at her cheeks and clearly trying to pull herself together. "I'm better now."

He gave her a little smile. "You don't need to be

'better,' or sorry, Jeannie. Just be how you are and that's enough. You can let yourself have feelings."

She nodded a little to show she heard him, but kept her eyes focused out the front window. "I'd like to get home, if that's okay," she said softly.

Gustavo hesitated, wanting to talk more about what she was going through, but decided this wasn't the time. He was sure she wanted to see her family in person and be sure everyone was okay. So he started the truck again and continued the drive toward her childhood home, neither of them speaking.

It was only when they were nearing the driveway that Jeannie spoke again. "I would like to visit Mr. Gibraltar tomorrow morning, if it's possible," she told him, her voice determined.

Gustavo glanced over at her for a moment before turning his eyes back to the road. "You want to keep digging into the books?" he asked.

Jeannie nodded, looking sure of herself and very serious. "I need to know what happened and, if the break-in was related, why they would do something like that. If you don't want to come with me, though, I completely understand—"

"Oh I'm coming, too," he said, cutting her off. "We'll figure it out faster together."

He didn't say that he couldn't let her continue this on her own, possibly putting herself in danger without him there by her side. She accepted his words without any argument, which was a relief. She just nodded and they drove the rest of the way in silence.

Gustavo parked his truck in front of the Lawson home and turned to her. "I'll call them as soon as I can and see if we can make a visit," he told her.

"And update me on what the police say," she said, biting her lip. "I want to know what they think happened at your place—if maybe this will make them push harder to find the thief and trespasser."

He agreed and she turned her gaze away to open the door, but stopped and looked at him with that look she got when something brilliant occurred to her. He waited to hear what it could be, wondering if she had come up with some new and amazing way to explain that book being found in his house.

"If you end up going back to your place, would you grab an old shirt? One you don't care about getting back, and ideally one that isn't washed," she said.

It was so unexpected that it took him several seconds to process it. He raised his eyebrows at her, waiting for more explanation.

"You'll see why," she said, giving him a little mischievous smile.

He laughed at that, and she smiled even wider. After all the anxiety of the past hour, it felt good to laugh, and the exchange was so reminiscent of the old days—the best times between them. It stirred his heart in a way he'd missed so much.

He twisted and reached into the backseat, feeling around until his fingers landed on fabric. "Is this okay?" he asked, pulling the torn shirt into the front.

"I tossed it back there when I ripped it and keep forgetting to throw it out."

"Perfect," she said, grabbing the shirt eagerly from his hand, their fingers brushing for only the briefest moment. He waited a beat, but when it was obvious she wasn't going to tell him anything more, he resigned himself to not discovering what she had planned until she was good and ready to share it with him. "I'll keep you updated on Mr. Gibraltar and the police," he said, sobering a little.

Jeannie nodded and opened the car door. Gustavo desperately wanted to lean across her and grab the door like he had earlier, look into her eyes with their faces only inches apart. He longed to stay close, to protect her and to experience more of her.

But then the door swung wide and the moment passed. She seemed to hesitate before she stepped out and he waited, hoping she would say something, give him a reason to spend more time with her, but then she stepped out and closed the door behind her and he was alone in the truck.

She gave him a little wave and he waved back, wanting something to say to her to prolong the moment, not ready to leave quite yet, but there was nothing he could do and he had to get back to Angie. So he watched until she was safely inside and then drove away, glancing in the mirror at the front door of her home, wishing he wasn't driving away from her.

He was still scared for their safety, but he also felt hope welling within him. There was still a spark between them; he could feel it and he was sure she could, too. The past wasn't dead for him, not by a long shot, and perhaps as they worked together to solve this case, she would see that they still belonged together.

Jeannette walked into the house, her nerves buzzing with anxiety at the unusual silence. She moved carefully, her heart in her throat, and found Beth in the living room, quietly working on a puzzle with Stella, pieces scattered all over the coffee table. Jeannette watched them as she told her body to relax and felt a tug on her heart. She wished she was part of that sweet scene instead of on the outside worrying about thefts and break-ins.

"Where is everyone?" she asked Beth, who hadn't noticed Jeannette enter the room. She hated the irrational fear still bubbling inside her. She knew that she'd checked in and everyone was fine only a few minutes ago, and that she could even see with her own eyes that Beth was calm and happy and safe, but she needed to hear it again.

Beth looked up at her with concern in her eyes. "Dad's in his workshop again, and you and I are under strict orders to stay out, but he wanted me to make sure you were okay. He's got Rachel and Carson in there helping him for a few minutes before they need to get to bed. He said he'd come check on you then. I think he's making some Christmas gifts for us. Everyone is fine. I promise."

Jeannette let out her breath, feeling the tension in her finally ease a little.

"What happened?" Beth asked. "We get this text from you and now you're standing there looking around like you expect somebody to jump out of the shadows. Did something happen while you were with Gustavo?"

Jeannette shook her head, not sure what to say. Finally she decided it was best to tell Beth the truth, even if it made her worry, too. "Someone broke into Gustavo's house. We don't know who or why, but it has me jumpy. I think it might have to do with the book."

Beth listened, her face serious. She absorbed this for a moment, then asked, "You think it was that important to someone?"

Jeannette shrugged. "It seems like too much of a coincidence that this happened the same day we went around telling a bunch of people about what we found," she said.

Jeannette wished she'd been a little more careful with the information about the book. Between the police station, CuriosCity and the library, a dozen people knew what they'd found and where, and who knew how far the gossip had gone after that?

"So you think this book is actually something special?" Beth asked.

Jeannette considered it seriously. "It really is," she said, "but it shouldn't be *that* special. Someone stole a few books, but they weren't even worth all that much. The University of Lexington isn't the Louvre or anything."

"So maybe it really was just a coincidence," Beth replied.

Jeannette knew this might be the case, but she couldn't seem to accept it. Her gut told her it was more than that.

Right that minute, though, she decided not to argue. "Hopefully, we'll figure out what happened tomorrow when we talk to Mr. Gibraltar, and everything will get back to normal," Jeannette said, though she really had no idea what normal might look like after all this, and now that Gustavo had reappeared in her life.

"Mr. Gibraltar? The man whose wife and son passed all those years ago?" Beth asked.

Jeannette turned to her sister, surprised. "Yeah, Gustavo bought his ranch. It's where he found the book. How do you know about that?" she asked.

Beth gave her a little smirk. "I've lived here my whole life, Jeannie. And I wasn't as lost in books as you were. I've paid attention. Mr. Gibraltar was a nice man, always pleasant at church. Sad, but kind."

Jeannette wondered if she had missed out on something by avoiding getting close to the people here and constantly planning her exit, rather than noticing the community. Then Jeannette realized Beth might actually have useful information and she sat beside her sister, pulse racing again at the possibility of a new lead. "Do you think he could've been the one to steal those books?" she asked.

Beth immediately shook her head. "He was a good man. Honorable. Did the best he could, always, even if it left him with almost nothing in his own pocket. His son was a bit wild, though, if I remember correctly. I could imagine him possibly doing something like that."

Jeannette shook her head. "He couldn't have," she explained. "Mr. Gibraltar's son died years before the theft."

Beth shrugged. "I always wondered how they knew when the books were taken. I bet some of them hadn't been looked at very carefully in a decade or more."

Jeannette was about to answer when she paused. She couldn't believe that had never once occurred to her. The theft could have been long before the actual discovery of it. She stared at her sister, eyes wide. "You're right," she said, shaking her head. "I can't believe I didn't think of that. And the police didn't, either. We all just assumed someone had made the switch recently or it would have been noticed, but really, that was the whole point of the fakes. So it *wouldn't* be noticed."

Another thing occurred to her. "I wonder if the kid's death was somehow connected to the thefts," she said, murmuring to herself.

"What do you mean?" Beth asked.

"Maybe he knew too much and someone decided

to get rid of him," Jeannette answered. If there was a murder involved, it would explain why somebody might care about them digging into the book thefts. Murder didn't have a statute of limitations.

Beth held up her hands, telling Jeannette to slow down. "Doesn't that sound like a bit of a stretch to you? It was a few books they stole, not diamonds. Those couldn't be worth enough to murder someone over, right?"

Jeannie shook her head. "They're worth maybe up to twenty grand for the rarest of the ones that were stolen. I remember the total was less than a hundred thousand dollars. But it seems like quite a coincidence that he stole a bunch of books, got away with it and then had an unexpected accident."

Beth gave her sister a very serious stare. "You don't have any proof, though, Jeannie, and I think you forget how small this town can be when it comes to gossip. Don't start going around saying Mr. Gibraltar's son was murdered because he was stealing books. Something like that could have ripple effects you haven't anticipated."

Jeannette nodded, recognizing the wisdom in her sister's words. If the break-in at Gustavo's was related to any of this, blabbing about a possible murder could be very dangerous.

She took a deep breath, feeling fear rising in her. What if she was putting herself in danger? Or worse yet, her family? "Maybe it would be better if I stopped looking into this," she said to her sister, dropping onto the couch, exhausted and defeated.

Beth added another piece to the puzzle and then turned to Jeannette. "That is one of the most ridiculous things I've ever heard you say. There was a theft, and if your guess is correct, a murder, too. You can't just let that go. Even if you stop now, you'll always wonder, and whoever did those things will still be out there."

Jeannette couldn't argue with any of that. Beth continued, "You're one of the smartest people I know, Jeannie. I believe in your ability to figure this out. Just, you know, check in with me sometimes. I can't believe you never thought the books could have been stolen years before," she finished with a little eye roll.

Jeannette smiled. "I'll definitely come to you for your sage guidance, Wise One," she said.

Beth nodded, looking satisfied. "Okay, on to other things. What's that you're holding? I've been curious about it since you walked in the door."

Jeannette had completely forgotten about the old shirt that now rested in her lap. Suddenly she was excited for a different reason.

She smiled at her sister. "I've got a project in mind. Do you still have that tub of stuff here from when you were really into quilting?"

Her sister nodded. "Mom was always so sure I'd want to start that up again once the kids were older," she said with a sad little smile as she got off the floor and stretched her body.

Jeannette's heart twisted a little. That was just like their mother, so optimistic and enthusiastic about her girls' passions. Jeannette was sure her mother believed until her dying day that Jeannette would be an author and rare book library curator. She would never believe her little Jeannie would be happy creating advertisements.

Jeannette pushed those thoughts away, as well as the ones about the break-in and the books and Gustavo, and she followed Beth into her old room. Jeannette's life was confusing, but in this moment, at least, she could ignore it and do something positive for someone else, and that thought was simple and good.

Beth pulled a large tub from the closet and opened the lid, and in no time at all, they had the things Jeannie needed for her project. Soon she was sitting on the couch sewing while Beth and Stella puzzled. She let the project and the soft talk of the mother and daughter take her mind off of everything but the moment at hand. It was all so soothing, almost meditative. Jeannette was by no means a professional when it came to stitching, but her skills met her needs and she was happy to have something to do with her hands after all the excitement of the day. She still couldn't believe it was just now dusk, with all that had happened.

After a few more minutes, Beth announced that it was bedtime. Stella ran to tell the others, and Beth sat beside her sister. "So, how was spending the day with Gustavo? Besides the scare at the end, I mean," she asked.

"It was busy," she said with a shrug. "We went to the police station, but they weren't any help. Then to CuriosCity and to the university library. Then we were going to see if there was anything useful in his house, but, you know…" she said, drifting off.

Beth gave her a quick squeeze. "That must have been so upsetting. I'm glad everyone was safe. Was Gustavo's family over at his mother's, then?"

Jeannette could tell what Beth was asking. "His mom was watching Angie. There's no mom in the picture," she said.

Beth leaned back against the cushions. "No wife, huh?"

"No wife," Jeannette repeated. "It's a long story and not really mine to tell, but Gustavo's raising Angie on his own."

Beth was quiet, but Jeannette answered the unspoken question. "It isn't going to be like that," she said. "Everything between us was a long time ago. We live across the country from each other and have moved on from all that."

As she said the last part, though, Jeannette knew she was telling a lie. She hadn't moved on, not even after all these years. And she wasn't completely sure Gustavo had moved on, either. It was unnerving to think about what might be if they decided to give it a shot.

"What do you think about this thing so far?" she

asked, holding up the object she'd been working on for the previous hour, trying to distract both Beth and herself.

"It's looking good!" Beth told her, looking very approvingly at Jeannette's stitchwork. "You need some felt buttons, though."

Before Jeannette could ask where on Earth she was going to get felt buttons, Beth had hopped up and disappeared into the hallway that led to the bedrooms. She was back in a flash with a large bag of buttons and began picking out ones she deemed acceptable.

"Why do you have a thousand buttons?" Jeannette asked.

Beth shrugged. "I'm a mom. You never know when you need a bunch of buttons."

Jeannette accepted this as a reasonable fact and took the proffered handful of buttons. As she looked at them, she saw what Beth meant. They would be perfect.

Gustavo wasn't sure why he was nervous calling Jeannette. Was he worried she would be upset about the information he had to share, or was it something else? Still, he pushed the button and held the phone to his ear, waiting for her to pick up. He'd only seen her an hour before, but when she answered, he felt a wave of relief to know she was okay. "Gustavo?" she said it as a question, sounding worried.

"Hi, Jeannette. I just wanted to tell you what the police said," he told her.

"Oh," she said, sounding immediately more relaxed. "Do they think it has anything to do with the stolen books?" she asked.

Gustavo grimaced, even though she couldn't see him. "No," he said, knowing how disappointed she would be. "They think it was a random break-in, that someone saw the dark house and took the opportunity. I tried to explain about the books, but they brushed it off."

He knew they had a point, but it still nagged at him. It seemed so unlikely that this would be nothing more than a coincidence.

"I have an idea about that," she said, and he pressed the phone tighter to his ear, wondering what she'd come up with. "What if Mr. Gibraltar's son stole the books with a partner, and the partner murdered him? That would give them plenty of reason to want to go through your house looking for evidence, and murder has no statute of limitations, right?"

Gustavo tried to wrap his head around this new idea. "But didn't he die before the thefts?"

"Not necessarily," Jeannette told him. "Those replicas could've been sitting on the shelves for years before they were discovered."

He immediately recognized the truth in those words. But other questions still nagged at him. "Why wouldn't they have broken in way back then if they thought there was incriminating evidence in the house? Why wait until people were actually on the scent and would be suspicious about it?"

Jeannie was silent for a moment, and he knew she was turning this over in her mind. "Maybe they did," she said. "Maybe they searched the house all those years ago and took whatever they could find, but they missed that book, and they got wind we found it so they wanted to look around to see if there was anything else they could find before we did."

It made sense, but seemed like a long shot. "It's possible," he said, not wanting to rain on Jeannie's parade.

"I know it sounds unlikely," she responded. "But this whole thing is pretty unlikely."

He couldn't argue, and she continued, "So I'd like to go back to the library tomorrow and look through the older logs. Maybe there will be something in there."

"Sure, we can do that before we visit Mr. Gibraltar, since we can't go there until eleven. How about I pick you up at nine?"

"Perfect, I'll see you then," she said, sounding like she was about to hang up the phone.

But there was one more thought he couldn't get out of his head. "Why would they make such a mess, though, Jeannie? They didn't need to do that."

"Maybe to make it look like a normal burglary, or—" She stopped, but it seemed like a more hesitant than thoughtful silence this time. "Or it could be a warning to us. To stop."

He didn't know what to say after that, and it seemed like she didn't, either.

"You should get some rest," Gustavo said. "I'll pick you up tomorrow and we'll try to figure all this out."

*Together*, he added silently. That made him feel better, at least.

# Chapter Six

Jeannette tried to sleep, but she couldn't seem to get comfortable. Every time she tried to drift off, she would think about Gustavo's ransacked house and her heart would start racing again. Finally, near midnight, she got up to make a sandwich. She hadn't eaten since that burger with Gustavo, and she hoped if she could get her stomach to quiet down, maybe her brain would, too.

She sneaked through the house, trying not to wake anyone, and then she heard a noise that made her freeze. A shot of adrenaline poured through her veins as she listened to the sounds. Somebody else was in the house, and her heart pumped as she reached for anything she might use as a weapon, but nothing came to hand. She chided herself for not being prepared enough and was about to retreat to her room to call the police when she noticed the slivers of light coming from the door that led to the kitchen.

Jeannette cautiously walked toward the door and looked through the slats, breathing a sigh of relief as she recognized her father's figure.

She pushed open the door and stepped inside the brightly lit kitchen, and he turned and gave her a little wave. "Would you like something to eat, sweetie?" he asked, moving toward the fridge.

"Dad, what are you doing up so late?" she asked, trying not to sound angry. He hadn't meant to scare the living daylights out of her, after all.

Mr. Lawson gave his daughter a sad smile, and her heart crumbled. Of course it was hard for him to sleep, alone in his room without his wife. She had been so focused on her fears that she'd forgotten how lonely he must feel every night.

"How about a sandwich?" he asked.

Jeannette sat at the kitchen table. "A sandwich would be great," she told him.

He bustled around and soon they were both eating. Jeannette hadn't realized quite how starved she had been and nearly inhaled her food, her father watching bemused. "It was quite a day for you, wasn't it?"

It had been such a tumble of excitement and disappointment, that even though she had told the whole story to Beth and her father, she didn't feel like either of them could really understand it.

Jeannette nodded. "It was exhausting, but I can't sleep. I'm scared, Dad," she confessed.

He took her hand and squeezed it. "Don't worry,

sweetie. You're safe, and I know you can figure this out," he said.

She tried to feel reassured, but his words didn't help much. She wasn't sure she would be able to solve this problem, and even less sure that they were safe. A creak outside made her jump, and Jeannette's head whipped toward the window.

Her father shook his head. "It's only the wind in the trees, Jeannie. I know how you feel, but in a few days you'll calm down and stop jumping at every little noise. I promise."

Jeannette considered asking him what he'd been through that made him know how she felt, but figured it was best not to ask for fear of bringing up difficult memories. He had enough of those in his head without her poking at him for more.

"I'm going to try to sleep," she said at last, stretching and standing. She gave her father a kiss on the cheek, put her plate in the sink and went back to her childhood room.

After a long while of staring at the ceiling, she finally drifted off.

The next morning, Jeannette stumbled into the kitchen in the morning in desperate need of coffee. Her father looked up from the eggs he was scrambling.

"Good morning, sweetie. Were you able to sleep?" he asked after pulling her in for a quick hug.

Jeannette didn't want to complain about the hours she spent awake, listening to sounds in the night. "I got some," she told him, but his skeptical look told her she wasn't fooling anyone.

"What's your plan for today?" he asked.

That was a question she could answer more easily. After all, she and Gustavo had discussed it last night and already texted that morning. "Gustavo and I are going to the library again, and then we're hoping to see Mr. Gibraltar. After that we will go to his house and see if there's anything there that might help us. And I should visit Linda and Henry since I promised them I would yesterday."

Her father nodded, looking thoughtful. "That sounds busy. I wish I could help you somehow," he said.

Jeannette walked up behind him and gave him a tight hug. "I know, Dad. I'll be back as soon as I can, and Gustavo and I won't take any unnecessary risks," she told him.

Her father looked into her eyes, pushing a strand of hair out of her face. "Try not to get hurt, sweetie," he said, and she knew he wasn't talking about the case.

Jeannette nodded. It would be too easy to fall back into a place where she could find herself with a broken heart again, and she had been through that enough.

She patted her father on the shoulder. "I will be careful," she told him. Then she went to take a few minutes to relax on the couch before she needed to get ready. As she settled into the cushions, though, she decided to try to get her mind off the mystery and the danger and Gustavo and instead do a little work. Maybe if she sent her boss some of the completed ad campaigns during vacation, management would be so pleased that she would get promoted in the spring rather than the end of the year.

A voice in the back of her head reminded her that she didn't need to work on it, even as a way to distract herself. After all, she had worked fifty-hour weeks for years and could take a little break from it now, to leave her computer closed.

But that nice apartment, that stability, that paycheck all had their say, too, so she pulled her computer out with a groan, turned it on and massaged her neck where the tension immediately began to build. She didn't like to admit it, but if Beth asked her right now if she enjoyed her job, it was very *very* obvious that the answer was no.

It was something she did because she was successful at it and it made a decent living, but if she was honest, she disliked every minute of it. Helping businesses convince people to buy things they didn't want and probably couldn't afford didn't fulfill her. She wasn't making anything better or more beautiful, wasn't improving the world.

And maybe she should think about that and consider finding a way to change something, but for now she needed to finish approving advertisements for overpriced luxury products. Jeannette leaned forward and clicked open one of the projects, looking through what her team had completed so far.

"Are you really trying to do work on your vacation?" Beth asked, leaning against the wall across from where Jeannette sat, her arms crossed as if she was mentally preparing a lecture.

Jeannette looked up guiltily, like she was a young child caught sneaking cookies. "I just have a couple projects to check over quickly. It'll only be a few minutes," she explained.

Beth shook her head. "You know how it affects you, right? You get all tense and unhappy and force yourself to do way more than you should so you can boost your paycheck. Just take a break, Jeannie. Enjoy your time away from all that for a little while. You've got enough stressful stuff going on here to fill up your days, I think."

Jeannette considered arguing, but she saw the plea in her sister's eyes and knew Beth was only trying to help. Reluctantly, she closed her laptop again and tucked it back under the couch. Beth walked over and sat beside her, looking pleased. "We should talk about what's going on with you and Gustavo," she said, sounding like a gossipy teenager.

"Actually, I should get ready," Jeannette said, glancing at the time. Her sister's expression was skeptical, but she didn't say anything. "Please keep everyone together today," she asked Beth. Jeannette needed the reassurance that her family would be safe while she was gone.

Beth's expression softened and she nodded, and Jeannette was able to walk away feeling a little better.

She showered and dressed, thinking about the thefts, about Mr. Gibraltar's son and what she might learn today. There were still so many questions, and the urgency of the situation gnawed at her.

There was so much she didn't know, but someone had to know *something*. Hopefully, Mr. Gibraltar could give them information to clarify what happened all those years ago.

By the time she spotted Gustavo's truck through the window, she was practically bouncing in anticipation, nervous and excited and scared all at once. She threw on her shoes and coat and left the house, taking a small bundle with her. She forced herself to walk rather than run.

As she crossed the distance to Gustavo's truck, she couldn't help but think of all the times in high school when she had run out to greet him as he drove up. This was so different, and yet so familiar.

Gustavo watched Jeannie walk toward his truck, thinking about how many times he'd seen her leave her house like this. He had always been thrilled to watch her coming to him, grinning at him, her hair flying behind her as she jogged his way. She wasn't grinning or running, but the familiarity still brought that rush of excitement as she covered the distance to his vehicle, despite his frayed nerves.

Jeannie pulled her coat tight around her, pressing some object to her stomach as she did so, trying to protect herself against the wind that had picked up that morning as it flung her hair around. She moved faster.

Gustavo looked up at the scattered clouds. There was no rain yet, but the wind held a hint of moisture and he hoped they would get a downpour one day soon. He loved the rain, and the place needed it. It had been a dry fall and rain would help him as he got the ranch running again.

Jeannie opened the door of the truck and slid inside, dragging the fingers of her unoccupied hand through her hair to settle it. She glanced into the back of the cab and saw Angie there. The smile she gave the little girl made Gustavo's heart jump.

"Hi, Angie! I brought something for you," Jeannie said, shifting in her seat to talk to her. "Do you want to see what it is?"

Angie's eyes lit up, and Gustavo felt his heart swell. Watching Angie and Jeannie interact made him feel as if he'd found everything that had been missing in his life. He couldn't help but feel a little hope that maybe the three of them could be a family one day, as unlikely as that was.

Gustavo leaned back in his seat to watch the interaction, wondering what it could be that Jeannie had for the little girl.

When Jeannie opened her arms and revealed the thing she had been carrying, his eyes widened in surprise.

It was him. A stuffed doll version of himself, wearing a shirt made out of the old, torn one Jeannie had taken the day before.

Jeannie spoke to Angie in a low voice. "This is a squishy Papa for you to have. He smells like your papa and everything. If your papa is ever not around and you need a hug, you can hug Squishy Papa. What do you think?"

Angie reached out as far as she could from her car seat and grabbed the proffered doll, pulling it close to her chest and squeezing it tightly. While she examined her new toy, touching the eyes and the shirt and the hair with her chubby toddler fingers, Jeannie watched and smiled affectionately.

Gustavo knew in that moment that he still loved Jeannie, as much as he ever had. He'd never stopped. He couldn't let her go again, not without being sure he'd done everything he could to be with her. He knew if he didn't try, he would regret it, just like he regretted those fifteen years they'd lost together.

Now wasn't the time to bring that up, but he would before she walked out of his life again.

"Skisshy Papa," Angie said, hugging it again and holding it out for her father to see.

"That's a wonderful gift, and I hope you will squish him lots and lots if I'm gone," he told the little girl.

"And he can be with you all night long, so if you are ever sad at night, you can get hugs before you go back to sleep," Jeannie added.

Gustavo looked at her in amazement, and she

blushed a little. It was clear she understood how much it meant to him to help Angie get over her night tantrums. He wanted to hug her tight and thank her over and over again for even trying.

"Soft," Angie said, petting the black curls on top of the doll's head. Gustavo looked closer and saw that they were fuzzy little buttons, sewn on to look like Gustavo's curly hair. "I sewed them on very tightly, but if you're worried about them being a choking hazard, I can make another one with yarn for hair instead. I have enough fabric and everything," Jeannie said as Angie's fingers ran over the little black bumps again and again.

"It's perfect," Gustavo said to her.

Angie pointed at Gustavo's head. "Like Skisshy Papa," she declared happily.

Gustavo laughed, and so did Jeannie. He wished this moment could last forever, and hated to break up the moment, but he was aware of the time passing and the important tasks for the day. "We should probably start the drive to the library. Do you want to hold Squishy Papa while I drive?" he asked Angie.

She nodded enthusiastically and hugged it tight against her. Gustavo reached back and pressed a hand against the little girl's curls before turning forward in his seat and turning the key in the ignition. "Thank you," was all he could say to Jeannie as she buckled her seat belt.

She nodded. "I hope it helps," she said softly.

Gustavo knew that it already had. The look of joy

on Angie's face was something to see, and she usually reserved that for only her closest circle of trusted people. If Jeannie could help show the girl that the world had lots of kind people in it who cared for her, she would be helping the girl more than Jeannie realized.

Gustavo pulled out of the driveway and they headed on the road toward the library. He glanced over at Jeannie and could tell she was both worried and excited, and he imagined she wanted to solve this mystery as quickly as possible. So did he, for that matter. He didn't want to take any more risks than was necessary.

"I talked to Mr. Gibraltar's nurse just before we left my mother's and she said he was having a good morning, but reminded me that it could change and we should try not to expect too much from this conversation. And the logs might not turn up anything useful, either," he said. He didn't want either of them to be disappointed if nothing came of their day.

Jeannie nodded. "No expectations," she agreed, though the clench of her jaw made it clear that she was desperately hoping for something that would get them closer to some answers.

He was, too. If any of Jeannie's thoughts about theft and murder were right, they were putting themselves at risk every day the mystery went unsolved. If the break-in wasn't a coincidence, someone out there knew what they were up to and didn't like it.

* * *

"Long time, no see," Brayden said with a smile as Jeannette and Gustavo walked toward the service desk. "You had such a great time yesterday that you decided to come back for more, is that it?"

Jeannette smiled at her old friend to hide any sign of worry or fear. "Hi, Brayden. Actually, I think I lost an earring in that back room. Could we go back there and search for it for a few minutes?"

Brayden looked a little disappointed. "I was hoping you were back with a new lead to the mystery— something exciting I could share at dinner parties," he told her.

Jeannette shook her head, trying to look disappointed herself. "No, we've only hit dead ends. I guess this case just wasn't meant to be solved."

Jeannette watched Brayden carefully, wondering if he would buy her act. She'd decided not to tell anyone at the library about any of the information they were after now, for fear it would put her and the people she cared about at risk. She had promised her father she'd be cautious, and she was going to do her very best to do so.

And that meant treating everyone as a possible thief and murderer, even sweet, friendly Brayden. After all, he had worked at the library all those years ago, and he could easily have gotten his hands on the real copies. Several of the employees still working there could have. She thought she knew these people, but did she? Did she really know anyone there, despite all the hours she had spent with them?

It was best to be friendly and try to get the information without much fuss, then get out of there as quickly as possible.

Brayden shook his head, looking even more disappointed. "I hope you're wrong," he said, then pulled out the bundle of keys from his hip and selected one. "Here. Be sure to lock it on your way out."

Jeannette felt a mixture of guilt, for lying to someone who seemed to trust her so much, and worry that Brayden had at some point over the years handed his keys to someone else—someone who had more nefarious intentions than she did.

She managed to avoid snatching the keys and running down the hall, instead continuing the ruse that there was nothing special in that room except a missing earring, with Gustavo following, holding Angie's hand as she bounded along near his leg. The sound of a child was soothing in the midst of all the stress, and Jeannette focused her attention on the little girl for a few moments, not on the task at hand.

As soon as she'd unlocked the door, however, she put her mind right back on the task at hand. After all, she wanted to move quickly and get out of there as soon as they could. The minute the door was closed, she went over to the log books and pulled two off the shelf—the one for the year Mr. Gibraltar's son was murdered, and also the year before that.

This time, instead of just looking through, Jeannette pulled out her phone and started quickly snapping photos of each page. Gustavo entertained Angie on the floor, keeping an eye on the door in case somebody decided to drop in unexpectedly, and in a couple of minutes, Jeannette was settling the ledgers back into place. She didn't have high hopes anything would come of it, but it was exciting to have one more possibility to pursue.

They left the room, and Jeannette slid the key into the lock, securing the door. Before she could pull the key back out, though, her phone beeped with a new message. She looked at Gustavo, fear gripping her. What if it was her dad or Beth? What if something had happened while they were gone? She could read worry in Gustavo's eyes, too, and she grasped at her phone to read the message.

STOP NOW

Just those two words, from a number she didn't recognize. Gustavo pulled out his own phone and tapped the number into a search, then shook his head. "That's a fake number," he told her in a quiet whisper.

Jeannette didn't know what to do, so she slid her phone back into her pocket with trembling hands and reached for the ring of keys, pulling it loose from the door. After another glance at Gustavo, who was holding Angie tight in his arms, she began walking down the hall, Gustavo falling into step beside her.

The three of them slowly headed back to the front

desk, Jeannette willing herself to act calm, to look relaxed. She couldn't let on how afraid she was.

"Did you find what you were looking for?" Brayden asked, his tone as chipper as always, when she handed him back the keys.

"Yep, thanks," she said, giving him a warm smile that she hoped would hide the feelings inside her. "Have a good rest of your day," she added as they started to walk away.

"You, too!" he called. "And don't be a stranger. Come by again soon!"

Jeannette could only wave, not trusting herself to say anything. She didn't know if she would ever come back here again. Suddenly her home away from home felt like a trap. She felt watched, as if every step she took was being analyzed, and if she wasn't careful someone would jump from the shadows and get her. Every nerve was on fire and it was only through sheer force of will that she made it to Gustavo's truck without breaking into sobs.

Once she was there, though, with the safety and privacy of the cab surrounding her, she let herself go, burying her face in her arms. Gustavo's arms wrapped around her, giving her a warm, secure cocoon in which to weather the storm. After a minute or two she felt a bit calmer and was able to take a few steadying breaths. She shifted and Gustavo moved away. She wanted to ask him to stay close, to keep giving her comfort, but she held back. It was better not to add that complication, she told herself, when things were complicated enough already.

"Sad," Angie said from her car seat in the back, and Jeannette turned to see the little girl holding out her doll, offering it to Jeannette.

Her heart melted, seeing Angie's attempt at comfort, and Jeannette gave the girl a smile. "I'm better, thank you," she said, patting the head of Squishy Papa.

Angie pulled the doll back tight against her body, looking relieved, and Jeannette gave a little breathless laugh.

"What do you want to do now?" Gustavo said, looking hard at her.

Jeannette met his gaze. "We need to solve this, now, or everyone I love will need to leave this town," she told him, hoping he understood that she meant him and Angie, too.

"Well," he said slowly, "it seems like there's only one thing to do. We need to solve this thing very quickly and get this dangerous person in custody."

She started to protest, but he cut her off by saying, "We've started this thing together, Jeannie, and I'm not going to feel safe until we've solved it and we know who tried to hurt us. Even if you leave and that's enough to make whoever did this go back into hiding, I can't constantly watch over my shoulder, wondering if they'll change their minds and try to tie up loose ends. I don't want to worry about Angie's life being in danger every time we take a walk downtown."

Jeannette didn't know what to say. Gustavo seemed so determined, and she didn't know how to argue with him, but she was so scared of him or Angie getting hurt, she couldn't bear it. Still, she understood his reasoning and he was smart enough to make his own decisions. "Fine," she said at last.

He nodded, satisfied, and buckled his seat belt. "Then let's go see Mr. Gibraltar," he told her.

They drove in silence for a few minutes. Gustavo had a hard time concentrating on the road, so many thoughts swirled in his head. He could see Jeannie's hands clenching and unclenching in her lap, and he wished there was something he could say that would help, but he had no words. He glanced at his mirrors over and over again, feeling as if they were being followed.

"Do you think we should call the police?" Jeannette asked finally, startling Gustavo out of his own thoughts.

He grimaced. After all the time he'd spent on the phone with them the day before—trying to convince somebody, anybody, to take the situation more seriously—he found it hard to believe a phone call would be worth the time, even with the anonymous text.

"I think we should try to gather a little more information first," he said. "Otherwise they'll brush us off again."

Jeannie nodded and looked at the phone in her lap. "He knows my phone number," she said, sounding shaken. "He knows where you live. I don't feel safe, Gustavo," she said softly.

"Neither do I," he confessed. "But I'm not going to feel safer because we give up now. That person is out there, and if we don't find out who it is, they will still know your number and where I live tomorrow, and there's nothing to stop them from harming us if they choose to."

Jeannie didn't say anything at first, and Gustavo wondered what she was thinking. Finally she looked out the window and took a deep breath. "What do you think we should say to Mr. Gibraltar?" she asked in an almost normal voice.

Gustavo had been considering just that. "I think if we talk to him about what his son was like, we'll find out if he has any information that might be useful," Gustavo said. "I don't think we should sound like we suspect his kid of anything illegal, or he might get offended or nervous and hold back valuable information."

Jeannie nodded, looking determined. "That sounds like a good tactic to me," she said. "We should also ask about the renter. We still can't entirely rule that out as a possibility."

Gustavo had totally forgotten about that. So much had happened in the past day that it made his head spin, and he had a gut feeling that Jeannie's guess about the son was the correct one. He trusted her deduction abilities, and her intuition.

"Right, the renter is still possible. Remember, though, he might not be able to tell us anything," he reminded her.

"Don't worry. I know this is a long shot," she said reassuringly, but her expression still didn't change.

Not that he had really expected it to. Jeannie wanted to figure out this mystery and he knew she would do anything she could to make that happen if it would keep her family safe, and rightly so. If Mr. Gibraltar couldn't share any information with them that day, it wouldn't dampen her resolve one bit. She wouldn't skip a beat and she would just come up with another plan, a different tactic. She had gotten a lot of her mother's intensity; it just came out a little differently than it did in Mrs. Lawson.

And he loved that about her.

He pulled into the parking lot of Great Oaks Care Estates and parked in a space near the building with OFFICE written above the door. There were several other buildings scattered around the grounds, all with matching blue exteriors. They were clearly housing for the residents. Gustavo stepped out and unbuckled his daughter, then held her hand as she walked beside him toward the door, her other arm wrapped around her new doll. He watched the parking lot carefully, searching for danger or anything out of the ordinary, but there was nothing.

He couldn't stop feeling on edge, though, and by the way Jeannie was glancing around, neither could she. Their eyes locked and he took a deep breath. She copied him, allowed her shoulders to loosen and relax and then they both continued toward the building.

As they walked, the first few raindrops were beginning to fall, and Gustavo wondered if it would be pouring by the time they came out. Angie's rain boots were still at his house, so she was in the tennis shoes she'd worn the day before, and he hoped they would be enough. He didn't have spare clothes for her, either, which added another little additional stress to an already incredibly stressful day.

He could have left Angie home with his mom, but he'd been too worried that something could happen while he was gone, so he brought her along despite the extra difficulties that would bring. Now he wasn't sure if that was the right decision, or if he'd put his daughter in even more danger. There was nothing he could do now, however, except keep a close eye on her, and he was certainly doing that.

They entered the office, where a young blonde woman took their information and walked them into the recreation room, pointing them toward the elderly man. He was sitting at a table working on a puzzle, moving the pieces around slowly, attempting to fit two together with stiff fingers.

Gustavo tried to stay calm, to not show how worried he was as they walked toward him. "Mr. Gibraltar? I'm Gustavo, this is Jeannie and this is Angie. I purchased your house. Thank you for agreeing to let me visit you today," Gustavo said, taking the old man's proffered hand and then sitting in a seat near him before placing Angie on his lap.

"I did, did I?" the old man said, looking confused for a moment. "Well anyway, it is good to have visitors, especially a little one," he said, smiling fondly at the little girl.

"Skisshy Papa," Angie said, hugging her doll tight and pushing herself closer to the real version.

Her reaction didn't seem to faze Mr. Gibraltar. "Do you like puzzles?" he asked her.

Gustavo could imagine her knocking everything onto the floor in her enthusiasm to help with the puzzle, and he tried to figure out a kind way to say it might not be the best idea when Jeannie piped up, "I think I see some crayons and coloring pages. Maybe Angie would like to color a picture?"

Angie nodded enthusiastically and Gustavo gratefully shifted so Angie was close to the table but not in arms' reach of the tiny puzzle pieces. Jeannie set paper and crayons in front of her and the girl began coloring furiously in big looping swirls.

Mr. Gibraltar laughed. "I miss little ones. I had a son who was such a firecracker at that age and I loved every minute of it. He died before he got old enough to settle down and have children of his own," the old man said with a sad shake of his head.

Jeannie and Gustavo's glanced at each other for

a moment, and Gustavo thought perhaps they would get the information they were looking for, after all.

And then maybe they would feel safe again.

"What was your son like?" Jeannie asked.

The old man launched into stories of his son as a young boy, getting into mischief like a child did. It was clear he doted on his son and Gustavo was glad he was there to hear the stories, to spend time with this man, even though his nerves still sang that time was of the essence and danger was near.

Mr. Gibraltar's eyes danced as he shared his memories, and Gustavo recognized the same kind of love he felt for the little girl in his lap. He prayed she would live a full and happy life. Once, Jeannie's phone dinged, and when he glanced at her, he saw her lips pinch tightly together and knew it was the anonymous texter again. But she swiped her phone to silent and looked back at the old man, her face expressionless. He admired her inner strength and felt a pull to protect her as much as he wanted to protect Angie. She was his family, too.

"He died too young, little Ricky," Mr. Gibraltar continued. "He got in some trouble he did, made some bad choices, but he was a good boy at heart. He would have come around. I know it."

Nobody said anything for a moment. Gustavo didn't feel right pushing the man for more details, even with how urgent it felt. Mr. Gibraltar had been through so much and Gustavo couldn't ask him to relive what must have been a terrible time.

But it seemed Mr. Gibraltar wanted to share, because he continued, "Something was going on with Ricky, that much was obvious. For months he hardly came out of his room, only popping out once in a while with that friend of his. Never liked him," he added, shaking his head.

"And then he fell when they were near the mine shaft, though why they were there only God knows."

"He fell in a mine shaft?" Gustavo asked, surprised. He had known it was an accident, but that wasn't what he expected. "That's how he…passed away?" he said, realizing at the last second to adjust his language so as not to upset the man.

Mr. Gibraltar looked so sad it made Gustavo's own eyes sting. "He survived the fall. Busted his leg up something awful, but we thought he would be fine in the end. He seemed a little thoughtful, a bit serious, but nothing so strange that we would worry. We put it down to the pain medication. And then that night, while we was sleeping…"

He trailed off, and Gustavo didn't have the heart to push. "What happened?" Jeannie asked softly, holding the old man's hand in hers.

"Brain swelling, they told us. Said he went in his sleep. Didn't explain how that necklace he was wearing got broken, though. Always wondered about that. Pieces scattered everywhere. Never did find the charm that had been on it," he said, drifting off again, as if he was reliving the image in his mind.

"I thought we had more time. He wouldn't tell us

what was happening. I should have made him tell me, but I thought that he would come around when he was ready, that maybe his mother would get it out of him. He was always so good to her, taking care of her more than a young man should need to when she was sick. Oh but that boy loved his mama. He wasn't yet eighteen," he added.

Angie wriggled in Gustavo's arms and he realized he'd been squeezing her as he heard the man's story, both from sympathy and curiosity. Who would murder this kid over a few books? Who would do something like that, hurt a family so much?

"After it happened I was so heartbroken I couldn't even go into his room," he said with a grimace.

"Who was Ricky's friend?" Gustavo asked, hoping to move the man away from the topic that seemed to be almost physically hurting him, and also hoping that perhaps he could get some information that might help put the case to rest.

Mr. Gibraltar shook his head. "I had nearly everything taken away, I did," he said. "Even the snow globe his mama gave him when he was as little as that girl is now. It was so pretty, with a big Christmas tree right in the middle and little skaters around it. I regret letting that go, but I went to the shop last week and it was too late. Sold," he said, looking as if he might cry.

Gustavo wondered how long ago that had really been, and his heart went out to the man who was living with so much loss.

"Our boy was a good one, Madeline," the old man said to Jeannie, grasping her hand tight and looking into her eyes. "We did the best we could. You were a good mama and don't believe one bit that it was our fault."

"Okay, Mr. Gibraltar," an attendant said, walking up behind the man. "It has been a long day. Let's get you back to your room for a rest now."

"I miss you, Maddie. Come back and see me," Mr. Gibraltar told Jeannie as he was led away, and Gustavo and Jeannie waved goodbye.

"I will," she said softly, even though the man was too far away to hear her.

Gustavo put an arm around her and squeezed her close to his side, holding Angie in his other arm. "Sad man," Angie said, and Gustavo nodded, looking over at Jeannie, whose eyes didn't leave Mr. Gibraltar until he was out of sight.

*Please, God,* he prayed, *help me find the words I need to say to her. I can't miss any more time with her than I have already.*

It was dim outside when they left Great Oaks despite it being just past noon. Dark clouds were blocking the sun and the rain was coming down heavily. Jeannette's heart was a mess of emotions she couldn't untangle. She was scared for herself and those close to her, but she also felt a deep need to know the truth of what had happened all those years ago. And she wanted to cry for Mr. Gibraltar and for his son and for Madeline.

"He'll see them again, you know," Gustavo told her, and Jeannette nodded.

As she climbed into the truck, she tried to think logically through everything Mr. Gibraltar had said, knowing she didn't have time to let emotions carry her away. "It's a terrible story, but we still can't be absolutely sure the boy was murdered."

She thought about how he'd grabbed her hand and called her Madeline in that fiercely loving way. "But I don't think Ricky Gibraltar could have done anything to hurt his family," she said.

Gustavo nodded and pulled the keys from his pocket. "I don't think so, either. There are still a lot of questions, but I don't think he was involved. I only wish we knew who his friend was. Mr. Gibraltar seemed to think he was bad news."

Jeannette started to nod, and then stopped as her mind made a connection it hadn't before. She let out a little "Oh!"

"What is it, Jeannie?" Gustavo asked, his voice hardly registering in her brain.

The realization sent a jolt through her, and she didn't know how she hadn't thought of it. Her phone, which she'd almost been afraid to touch a moment ago, was in her hand in a blink and she was scrolling through the pictures she'd taken that morning.

Yep, there. And there.

Jeannette crumpled into a ball as the weight of

the knowledge crashed on her, her head resting on her knees in the cramped space of the cab. "Oh no, oh no," she mumbled.

"Jeannie, talk to me," Gustavo said, sounding worried.

"I know who it is," she said in a whimper.

## Chapter Seven

She felt a warm hand squeezing her shoulder, and it brought her out of herself a little. She turned to see Gustavo watching her, his face full of concern and worry. She almost didn't want to tell him what she knew, didn't want to make those furrows even deeper, but she needed to share this burden.

"It was Anthony," she said at last.

"The police officer?" he asked, as if there might be another Anthony she was talking about.

Jeannette nodded without lifting her head off her legs. "He was Ricky's friend. I can't believe I didn't remember that. We only dated for a couple weeks, but they were friends. We all hung out once, near that old mine shaft. They liked to go there to smoke."

Gustavo was watching her carefully, as if he didn't totally believe it. "Just because they were friends and Anthony is a jerk doesn't mean he's a thief and a murderer," he said hesitantly.

Jeannette shot up in her seat. She needed him to see it, too. She spoke, her words fast and clipped. "Gustavo, it was him. He was Ricky's friend. I probably talked to them about the rare books at the library and the two of them used that information to steal those books. He knows we found the book, and he's been trying to stop us from digging deeper. He told us as much when we were at the police station. He even knew the thefts were almost twenty years ago, because he was the one who actually stole the books."

"Jeannie, that's a big leap," Gustavo said, his voice gentle.

She showed him a picture on her phone, pointing to one of the names on the log books. "Look! It's on another page, too. Anthony went to the library, Gustavo. He was there at least twice, maybe more if I search through all the photos."

Gustavo took the phone and stared at the name. "Anthony Pinker, right there," she said to him. "That was a couple months after he and I dated."

He looked at her. "Okay, so we know he was friends with Ricky, we know he went to the library and we know that he knows we've been trying to solve the old case," Gustavo said. "That's not enough."

"I know it was him," she said firmly.

Gustavo nodded. "I believe you. But we don't have any real proof. He can say he went to the library to research for a project or something, and I'm sure we can't get access to his financial records or anything from back then. Plus, he's a cop, it's not like we can go to the police asking them to suspect another officer of murder with no evidence."

Jeannette knew he was right. "We need to get some," she said, wondering how they were going to do that.

"Let's go back to my house," Gustavo said with a little grimace. "He obviously thought there might be something there that could incriminate him, or connect him to Ricky and put us on the trail."

Jeannette understood how he felt. She didn't really want to go to that house either, not with Anthony watching them and the knowledge that he got in once.

Or maybe twice.

Jeannette turned to him. "Do you know how the break-in happened? How he got into the house?"

Gustavo nodded. "There was a window that wouldn't shut all the way. I hadn't had time to fix it yet, but you better believe I'll be doing that as soon as this is all over."

Jeannette could see the uncertainty in his eyes and her heart broke for him. He had just moved into his home, and now here he was wondering if he would need to leave again to keep him and his daughter out of harm's way. They *needed* to solve this and make Colby safe for that sweet little girl.

"Was it a window in the second bedroom?" she asked.

Gustavo seemed to realize where she was going. "Yes, it was. It looked like it had been broken for years," he said.

"So that could've been a way for Anthony to get in and out of Ricky's room without being noticed. To pass along materials or books or—"

She gulped, struggling to get out the next part. "Or to kill his friend when the fall didn't," she said at last.

Gustavo was silent for a minute, then said, "Did you want to see Henry after we search the house? It might be pretty late by that time."

Jeannette rolled her eyes up to the roof of the truck. "I completely forgot about that," she groaned.

Gustavo shrugged. "Do you think it's that big of a deal? Can't you go tomorrow?"

Jeannette shook her head. "Henry remembers. If you tell him you're going to do something and you don't, it breaks his heart. I'll call and let him know I'm not coming, but I will soon," she said.

She picked up her phone gingerly, as if it was dangerous, but it didn't make a sound and soon she was calling Linda.

"Hello?" Linda answered, sounding a little flustered.

"Hi, Linda," Jeannette said. "I need to tell Henry I'm not going to make it today. Can you put him on?"

Linda hesitated for a second, as if she wanted to ask questions, but then she said, "Hold on," and Jeannette could hear her calling Henry over.

"Hi!" Henry said into the phone.

"Hi, Henry, it's Jean-Jean," she said.

"Jean-Jean! Are you coming over now?" he asked excitedly.

Jeannette wished she could give him a different answer, but this was too important to put off. "I'm sorry, Henry, but I can't today. I promise I will come over soon and see you, though," she said.

"Oh," he said, sounding disappointed.

"I will see you soon," she told him again.

"Okay," he answered, still not his normal happy self. "See you soon."

There was a click and the line went dead.

Jeannette set down her phone and leaned back, hoping she had told him the truth.

Gustavo drove through the heavy rain, the windshield wipers slapping it away as best they could. He didn't want to go back to his house, but they needed to see if anything was there. They were running out of time—that much was clear.

As if to highlight that point, Jeannette's phone dinged. They both glanced at it for a moment before she finally picked it up and looked at the screen.

"Same number?" he asked.

"It says 'LEAVE TOWN NOW,'" she told him.

He didn't know what to say to comfort her, so he kept driving in silence.

"Maybe I should," she said at last, as they pulled into the driveway and Gustavo parked. "Leave, I mean," she added.

Gustavo could see that she was close to tears. "If you leave, it doesn't mean the rest of us will be safe here," he said. "If you go, we should all go."

"I don't know if my family can, or even will," she told him.

He understood what she meant. This was their home, had been for decades. They might prefer to live in danger rather than move somewhere else. "Maybe it can be temporary. Get away for Christmas and go from there," he said.

"Okay," she said. "Let's see if we can find anything here, and if it isn't enough..."

She trailed off, but he understood. He turned around in his seat to look at Angie and saw that she'd fallen asleep during the drive, clutching her Squishy Papa. It made him smile. All this worry and fear circulating around and she could rest, feeling safe with her new doll in her arms.

He got out and very carefully extricated his daughter from her car seat. Jeannette held an umbrella she'd found in the truck over them, and together they managed to get Angie inside without her waking up.

After Jeannie cautiously walked through the house to make sure it was empty, Gustavo took

Angie into the main bedroom and settled her into bed carefully, then went around to double check that every window in that room was locked. He felt as if every nerve was on high alert as he moved around, and once he was sure the room was secure, he turned on the baby monitor.

Normally he didn't use the monitor, but today he wanted to hear every little sound in that room while he and Jeannie conducted their search.

He left the room and carefully shut the door, then gestured at Jeannie to follow him into the smaller bedroom. They stood together in the doorway, looking around. There hadn't been much in that room to begin with: an old chair, a small shelf and the new bed he'd ordered for Angie, but each object had been moved around and knocked over. "He could have just searched and left it all the way he'd found it," Gustavo said.

"Unless he wanted us to know someone had been here. To make us back off," Jeannie answered.

Gustavo felt a shiver in his spine and went right to the window. "This never latched," he said, pushing the window all the way open, looking around outside carefully as he did so. "I didn't think it was that big of a deal when there were so many repairs to make," he added, feeling guilty.

Maybe if he'd fixed that first, some of this could've been avoided.

"Hey," Jeannie said softly. "If you'd fixed it, he

would have gotten in another way. I'm sure he's perfectly capable of breaking in a door."

Gustavo nodded, but he still couldn't help feeling guilty. He looked at the window frame, trying to see what was preventing the window from closing fully. It looked normal to him, but he wasn't an expert. He was starting to wonder if they would need to call in a real handyman when he noticed something in the bottom corner of the frame.

"Look here," he pointed at the nail head sticking out. It was painted white like the rest of the frame and only stuck out a couple of centimeters, so it was hardly noticeable, but it was enough to keep the window from closing tight enough to latch.

Jeannie leaned across him to get a better look, and he felt the warmth of her against him. He wanted so desperately to protect her, to be with her. Gustavo vowed in that moment to do so for the rest of his life, if she let him.

Jeannie leaned back and looked in his eyes. "So we know why the window wouldn't latch. I imagine they did that so they could sneak in and out without needing to leave the window fully open, or to stop Ricky's parents from shutting them out," she said.

Without thinking, Gustavo leaned over and brushed his lips against hers, resting his hand against her soft cheek. Even that light touch was enough to make the blood rush through him, remind him of what he'd been missing all these years.

When he moved away again, she was staring at him, looking shocked. Suddenly he felt embarrassed. "I'm sorry," he said, taking his hand away from her face and stepping back to give her some space.

"We can't talk about this now," she said in a rush, as if she didn't have enough breath to speak normally.

Gustavo felt awful for making her uncomfortable, but she moved away from him and wouldn't look at him, so he kept his words to himself. "Look around for clues," she said, her eyes on the floor.

Gustavo wasn't sure what they might find that Anthony had missed, but he started looking anyway.

They searched the walls and the floors, knocking on each board to discover if any were loose, indicating a possible hidden compartment, but found nothing. They even tore open the bottom of the chair to see if they could find anything inside, but there was nothing. They worked in silence, the air hanging heavy around them. At one point, Gustavo attempted to use Angie's magnifying class to study a spot more closely, but even that was unsuccessful.

After a half hour, they sat on the floor, disappointed. "I don't know what we're going to do," Jeannie said at last.

Gustavo knew what their only option was, and he could see from her expression that she did, too. He was about to say it aloud when she glanced around once more, as if desperate for some other possibility.

"We didn't check the baseboards," she said at last, determined to leave no stone unturned.

Gustavo didn't comment, not wanting to discourage her, even if he'd given up on finding anything that could be important enough to make a case against Anthony Pinker. He shifted onto his knees, his body aching from spending so much time on the floor, and started examining the baseboards. He saw Jeannie using her phone's flashlight to look inside the crack between the floor and the baseboards and he did the same.

For a few minutes, they searched, the room quiet, and then Gustavo spotted something. "Hey, Jeannie," he said softly. "Come look here."

She scrambled over and shone her light at the same place as his, and he could tell she saw the tiny glittering thing, too. "It's probably nothing helpful," he said, not wanting her to get her hopes up. "But I'll grab some tweezers and we can see what it is."

He stretched and walked away, feeling the tension in his body as he moved. There had been so much anxiety—so much watching their backs every moment—that he felt like a ball of live wires. He wondered if he'd ever feel calm again, ever feel like the people he loved were no longer in danger.

He came back with the tweezers, relieved to see Jeannie still there in the same place. Even being out of view for a few seconds had been enough to make him nervous. And the look she gave him made it clear she'd felt the same.

They couldn't go on like this much longer, he knew.

Gustavo sunk to his knees again and carefully pried the object out of the crack while Jeannie kept her flashlight trained on the spot so he could see. It popped out and rolled along the floor, and Jeannie lunged after it. She came back holding a small glass bead. It was silver and blue, and looked as if it had come from a bracelet.

Or a necklace.

From how sad Jeannie looked, he knew she had guessed the same thing. "Ricky Gibraltar's necklace broke the night he died," Jeannie said. "This piece probably rolled there and has been stuck ever since."

Gustavo stared at it. It wasn't enough to solve the case, but it was beautiful and very sad. "Maybe we can bring it to Mr. Gibraltar. See if he wants to have it."

Jeannie nodded and closed her fingers around the tiny thing. Just then they heard a noise from the baby monitor. In a flash they were both up and moving, rushing into the room and searching for any danger.

But the sound had only been Angie turning over as she woke up, and now she looked at her father with a sleepy pout. Once Gustavo was sure nothing was wrong, he knelt beside his daughter and brushed her hair away from her face. "Hi, baby. Ready to get up?"

Angie groaned and wiggled off the bed into his

arms, still not fully awake. Gustavo turned to Jeannie. "I think we should probably go," he said. "There's a pile of old papers over in that desk we can grab, and I'll get a bag of things together."

Jeannie nodded, went to the desk and started gathering any papers she could find while searching the drawers carefully in the process. He grabbed a duffel and started tossing a few clothes in with one hand for himself and Angie, wondering if he'd ever be back in this house. He went into the closet and took the file with his important documents, including his passport and Angie's birth certificate, just in case.

Soon they had everything they needed, and after a couple of trips, it was all in the cab of the truck. It wasn't quite dinner time, but the sky had gotten dark and the rain was coming down in sheets. Once they were in the truck, Gustavo looked at the pile of things. This might be all he would keep from that house. *His* house.

He turned and studied it through the rain. He'd been so happy to move there, to have a real home. And now it looked ominous, as if something dangerous might be hiding there. He felt a shiver along his spine.

"Hold on," Jeannie said from the passenger side, breaking into his thoughts.

She took the keys from his hand, and before he could say anything, she was out of the truck and running back to the house. He watched as she unlocked the front door and disappeared inside. A light in the living room lit up the front windows, making the house look like a home again, and he felt his heart squeeze tight.

Then the light was off and Jeannie was on the porch again, locking the door and then jogging to the truck, her hair wet and sticking to her. She climbed back in and held out her hand. Nestled in her palm was the little angel ornament he'd gotten for Angie from CuriosCity. That felt like so long ago.

He tried to say thank you, but no words came out. Jeannie didn't seem to need them. She placed it carefully in the top of the duffel and put on her seat belt. "We should get on the road," she said.

He took the keys and started the engine. "Am I dropping you off at your house?" he asked, reluctant to be away from her for the night.

She pursed her lips and he could see she was unhappy with that arrangement, too. "Would you and Angie be willing to have a sleepover at my dad's house? There's enough room, and then you and I can talk about what comes next," she said.

He knew what came next, as hard as it was to fathom. But the idea was appealing. He didn't want to be away from her, to spend another night worrying if she was okay. There was one problem, though. "My mom," he said to Jeannie. "I don't want her in that house all alone."

Jeannie thought for a moment. "Would she come,

too? It might be important that we have a discussion with all the adults," she said.

Gustavo shrugged. "I can see," he said.

Jeannette waited while Gustavo spoke on his phone in rapid Spanish, the occasional English word tossed in. She didn't understand most of it, but could tell Mrs. Rodriguez was reluctant to pack a bag and stay overnight at somebody else's home.

When Gustavo hung up, Jeannette waited to hear what the verdict was. He gave her a little smile. "She thinks it's silly, but she will meet us at your father's house and at least stay for dinner and a chat," he said.

Jeannette could tell he was relieved and so was she. He began to drive and she sent a quick text to her father, letting him know to expect company. She knew Gustavo's mom would be more than welcome, and hopefully her family's kindness would be enough to convince her to stay.

And then they could make the difficult decisions about what to do next, together. She still couldn't believe any of this had happened.

"How could Anthony be doing all these terrible things?" Jeannette said, trying to wrap her mind around it all. "How could he kill his friend over some money, and threaten us like this? Stealing books is one thing, but hurting other people? He couldn't have made more than a hundred thousand dollars from it."

She didn't understand it. As much as she had hated

being poor as a kid and hadn't wanted her family to lose their house, she couldn't imagine ever being so desperate as to kill someone for it. And from what she knew about Anthony and his family, he hadn't been desperate at all.

"Maybe it wasn't just about the money. Maybe it was something the two were doing for money, but then Ricky became a danger to Anthony somehow," Gustavo said.

Jeannette thought about that. "That makes sense. Mr. Gibraltar seemed so sure Ricky was a decent kid at heart. Maybe he's a doting father, but if he was right, Ricky could have decided to admit what he'd done, but if he did then Anthony—"

She stopped talking as she noticed the car coming at them, going much too fast for the small road, their brights on, horn blaring. Her breath caught in her throat as she realized the vehicle would crash right into them if Gustavo didn't do something fast.

He turned the wheel hard to the right, tires skidding on the slippery wet road. Jeannie reached for the grab handle and clutched it tight as the truck went off the road, splashing through the muddy puddles and breaking brush. Gustavo slammed on the brakes and soon the truck had stopped—tilted sideways with two tires on the pavement, two off. If they had gone just a little farther they would have hit the creek, possibly flipping the vehicle. Jeannette put her hand to her chest to assure herself that her heart was still right where it should be and still beating.

Gustavo turned in his seat, looking frantic. "Angie!" he shouted.

Angie was crying hard, and Jeannie ripped off her seat belt so she could reach the little girl. "Angie, what hurts?" Jeannie asked, attempting to sound calm even though her blood was rushing in her ears as panic welled up inside her.

"Skisshy Papa!" Angie shouted, reaching out her arms.

Jeannie was confused for a second before realizing what had happened. As the truck careened off the road, Angie's doll had slipped from her hands and fallen to the floor. That was what had upset her.

Jeannie pushed her body over the seat and reached down, feeling for the floor of the truck until her hand touched felt buttons. She grabbed the doll and set it into the little girl's lap. Angie giggled and hugged it close, happily oblivious to the danger she had been in.

Jeannie slid back into the front seat, relieved. She turned to Gustavo and managed "Angie's fi—" before Gustavo's arms were around her, hugging her tight.

Without thinking, she wrapped her arms around him. They were all alive, and they were together. She could feel tears streaming down her face. "I missed you," she whispered.

"I missed you so much, Jeannie," he said in her ear.

They stayed like that for a long moment before Jeannie pulled away, wiping at her cheeks. "We need to get home now," she said.

She looked around for the other vehicle, but the road was deserted. Still, she felt as if they were being watched. As if they were always being watched. She looked into his eyes and knew he was thinking the same thing. "We need to leave Colby," she said finally, feeling like crying again for another reason. "You, me, Angie, our families. All of us. It isn't safe here."

Gustavo nodded without argument. It had been unspoken between them all day, but now here it was: the time to face it. Jeannette felt more fragile than she had in a very long time, and she carefully checked that her seat belt was secure before Gustavo put his hands back on the steering wheel. She could see that they were shaking a little, and she didn't blame him.

Still, he maneuvered the truck back onto the road, his expression serious, and they drove the rest of the way to her house in a tense silence, both of them watching out the windows for danger. Jeannette held her breath every time another car went by, but eventually they were pulling into the driveway of her father's house, and Jeannette sighed, relieved. She could see her sister through the front window, playing with Stella. They looked happy and warm and safe, and Jeannette couldn't wait to hug them all close.

Her phone dinged and she felt the fear rise in her again. She looked at the screen.

"What does it say?" Gustavo asked, sounding re-signed.

"It says 'IT WILL BE WORSE NEXT TIME.'"

Gustavo didn't respond, just looked at her, his eyes sad. She opened the text and wrote a quick reply. She could feel him looking over her shoulder and felt the squeeze of approval.

No more. We give up. We're leaving, she wrote.

A message came back almost immediately. Good. I'll be watching.

She looked out the window as she felt a mix of emotions. Hope, disappointment, anger, fear and love all bounced around inside her as she watched her family playing happily in their home. She heard the crunch of gravel and jumped.

"It's my mom's car," Gustavo said, and Jeannette relaxed a little. She watched the car pull in beside the truck and everyone got out and dashed into the house.

Beth and her father and the children rushed to the door, and soon everyone was greeted and hugged, and Jeannette and Gustavo were settled on the couch with warm tea in their hands as everyone else finished making dinner.

Jeannette couldn't believe it was just now dinner-time. Her day felt like it had lasted eons. She sipped her tea, trying to stay calm when every creak made her jump. Gustavo, sitting beside her, took her hand in his and squeezed it tight. "It's okay now, Jeannie. We're here. We're safe. Everyone is safe."

She nodded, unable to answer. The panic she had tamped down earlier was rising to the surface, coursing through her entire body, overwhelming her. She put her tea on the table with a shaky hand and took deep breaths. "We could have died, Gustavo," she said, the reality of the situation hitting her.

Gustavo set down his drink and wrapped both arms around her. "But we're safe now, Jeannie. And maybe he'll leave us alone now."

"Maybe," she repeated, glancing out the window into the dark night, feeling watched.

Gustavo reached over and pulled the curtains shut, which helped her feel less exposed, but didn't completely ease her fear. She saw the car lights glaring into her eyes again, felt the truck swerving off the road and wondered if she would ever feel safe again. She could feel her entire body shaking.

Gustavo held her tighter, his arms strong around her, and she tried to focus on his touch, not the fear. There was only one way she knew to get through this moment.

"Will you pray with me?" she asked.

He said nothing and shifted away, and for a moment she missed his arms around her, but then his hands took hers and their foreheads touched. She looked into his eyes for a moment before closing hers. She tried to think of what to say, her mind still in the grip of her fear.

Gustavo's voice began, a soft rumble that she felt down to her soul. "Dear Lord, please help us know what to do. Please keep us and our families safe. We trust You and will be brave with You by our sides."

His words calmed her, and she sat there long after he finished speaking. When she opened her eyes, she felt a bit better, her heart not beating quite so hard anymore. "Thank you," she said to him.

Gustavo's eyes looked deep into hers. He said, "Thank you for being here with me, Jeannie. I'm so sorry I brought all this into your life, but there isn't anybody else I'd rather be with at this moment."

Jeannette felt her heart warm in her chest. She felt the same way. They sat like that—foreheads touching, hands clasped together—for a long while.

"I can't let you disappear from my life again," Gustavo said, his voice soft and serious as he looked into her eyes. "Not ever. It was the biggest mistake I've ever made, Jeannie."

He pulled her into another embrace, and she wrapped her arms around him, holding him close and breathing the smell of him in as her cheek rested against his shirt. She pushed any thoughts of the danger or the future away and let herself be in that moment. She breathed deep and let it go, feeling the tension she had carried for so long, for her whole life, ease a little.

And then Angie's happy voice came loud from the hallway, catching their attention. They broke apart as Beth came in with the girl, who was dressed in footed pajamas. They were bright blue and covered in cartoon bears. "Monkeys!" Angie shouted as she threw herself into her father's lap, showing her father the new pajamas excitedly.

Beth shrugged. "She insists that the pajamas are covered in monkeys," she explained.

Gustavo didn't miss a beat. "Those are some great monkeys," he told the little girl, who beamed with pride over her new monkey pajamas. "Where did these come from?" he asked, turning his eyes to Beth while he hugged his daughter close.

"I have a bunch of things in bins from when mine were that little and I thought Angie might want something special for her sleepover," she explained.

Jeannette watched the little girl giggle in her father's lap, and she felt happier. *Maybe this could work*, she thought. She wondered what their lives would look like now, but found she didn't really care, as long as they were out of danger and they were together.

Then it was time for dinner, and she found herself sitting at the crowded table with her father, Beth and her children, Gustavo's mother and Angie who was settled on Gustavo's lap. Jeannette was sitting in an office chair brought in so there would be enough seats. If her mind wasn't filled with worries and hard decisions, if life was just a little different, it would be the most beautiful moment—everyone together like this.

As it was, she could hardly taste the food or hear the conversation. Her mind was filled with what had happened and what might have happened and why. She tried to act as normal as possible, but she felt like a body going through motions while her mind was someplace entirely different.

It was only after Angie was settled into a makeshift bed on Jeannie's bedroom floor—with Squishy Papa, the nighttime routine was tear-free, despite the events of the day—that she felt free to speak about what had happened that day. The adults gathered in the living room while Beth's kids played elsewhere, the occasional shouts and laughs and crashes filtering in.

Mr. Lawson, Mrs. Rodriguez and Beth settled on the couch, while Jeannette and Gustavo stood. Suddenly Jeannette felt like she was giving a presentation.

And in a way, she was. She needed to get everybody to listen and understand if she was going to keep them safe. "We need to leave Colby," she said "All of us. Immediately."

She got exactly the reaction she expected. Beth had her eyebrows raised as if the idea was ludicrous, her father was shaking his head in a confused and defiant *no*, and Mrs. Rodriguez started speaking to her son in quick Spanish that Jeannette couldn't understand.

Gustavo held up his hands to stop the protests. "We know, but it's not safe here anymore. That book we found has made somebody very angry, and they've broken into my house, sent us threatening messages and run us off the road. They won't stop, and if they get desperate enough, they might try to hurt you, too."

Jeannette could hear the plea in his voice and felt guilt wash through her. "I've endangered everyone's lives by digging into this book thing," she confessed. "I'm so sorry."

Gustavo turned to her, looking shocked. He grasped her hand tight between his. "Jeannie, no. I brought this into your life, remember? The book was in my house. I brought it here. You didn't do anything wrong."

Jeannette was shaking her head long before he finished. She had known he'd say that. "I was the one who went to the police station with the book and set this whole thing in motion. It never occurred to me that I would be putting our lives at risk, but that is exactly what has happened."

"This is nobody's fault but the person who committed the crime," Mr. Lawson said. "And you know who this person is?"

Jeannette began to nod while Gustavo said, "We think we do, but we don't have any real evidence. Certainly not enough to have him arrested. And he's

a police officer, which makes things more complicated."

"Who do you suspect?" Beth asked, leaning forward.

"Anthony Pinker," Jeannette said.

Beth immediately started shaking her head.
"That's crazy. I know he was wild when he was a
kid, and you had a bad experience with him, Jeannie, but he really turned his life around. Does a lot
of good for the community. One of his friends died
and he took it to heart, totally changed. It's a very
sad story, actually."

"That friend of his was Ricky Gibraltar, and we
think he had a hand in his death. We don't know this
for sure," Jeannette said, cutting off Beth's protests,
"and we don't have time to get more evidence because the person who did it is doing anything they
can to stop us, and we don't know if that means they
would hurt our families, but it sure seems like it."

She could see they still weren't convinced.
"Please, come with us," Gustavo said. "I will buy
us all tickets for tomorrow and we'll rent a big place
somewhere and have a nice Christmas away and then
we can figure out next steps. Please," he repeated.

Jeannette waited, holding her breath. She wasn't
sure what she would do if they decided to stay.

The three adults on the couch looked at each other,
then back to Jeannette and Gustavo. "Okay," Beth
said at last, "I'm in. We'll be ready to leave tomor-

row. But choose someplace fun," she added. "With mountains and a lot of snow. If I'm not going to be home for Christmas, I might as well learn to ski."

Mrs. Rodriguez nodded. "I will need to go home and pack," she said, standing.

"Will you please stay the night and pack tomorrow?" Gustavo asked her. "I would feel much better if we were all together, *Mamacita*."

Her expression went soft and she agreed, giving her son a hug. Jeannette felt her heart starting to beat normally again. This was going to work.

"Wait a minute," her father said, sounding stern. "I have something to say."

Jeannette turned to him, praying he wouldn't argue more. She was so tired.

He held up two fingers. "I will go on two conditions. The first, you need to not complain when your Christmas present is late," he said, pointing at Jeannette.

Jeannette smiled. "I promise," she agreed.

"Second," he continued, "tomorrow is Sunday and I want to go to church. The same church I've attended for nearly fifty years. After that, we can fly off to wherever you want to go and I won't say a word."

Jeannette glanced at Gustavo and he shrugged. "We will take an afternoon flight. Everybody good with someplace snowy?" she asked.

Everyone was, and Jeannette slumped on the floor, exhausted, every ounce of energy gone now that she knew they would all be safe.

"Now that all that's settled, we should play cards," her father announced, sounding almost cheerful.

Jeannette looked at him in amazement. The idea of playing cards seemed ridiculous with all that was happening, and yet it also sounded absolutely wonderful.

Beth stood. "I need to take care of my children and whatever that crashing was earlier. You play without me."

Mr. Lawson turned to Gustavo's mom. "That makes four. Do you play spades?"

She smiled, her eyes sparkling. "I do, yes," she told him.

"Then let's go show these kids how it's done," he said, ushering her back into the dining room.

Jeannette looked at Gustavo, wondering what had just happened. He shrugged and said, "It's been a long time since we've played spades together. Do you still bid like a madwoman?"

Jeannette put on an expression of mock indignation. "I bid perfectly, thank you very much. You were always so conservative. You have to take a little risk sometimes."

"I agree," he said, looking serious. "But there are times when you need to play it safe."

She nodded solemnly, the joking attitude breaking apart as quickly as it had come. They'd taken a lot of risks lately, and they hadn't paid off. Now it was time to play a more conservative game.

Gustavo held out his hand to help her stand, and together they walked into the dining room and sat at the table, where Gustavo's mom was already sitting, shuffling a deck of cards. Her father was seated across from her, so Gustavo and Jeannette sat across from each other, partners for the game.

They played the game without much talking other than bids, and Jeannette tried to enjoy the break, though every few minutes a spark of fear bit at her. She would keep them all safe, she told herself. They would leave town the next day and find a way to have happy, normal lives. Right this moment, though, there was nothing she could do, and she wanted to spend an hour being close to the people who were so important to her.

# Chapter Eight

After the game was over, Gustavo said goodnight to his mother—who Mr. Lawson insisted take his room—and Mr. Lawson—who would be sleeping on an air mattress in the den—and then turned to Jeannie with a little smile, attempting normalcy. "You've gotten better," he told her, then added, "but you still bid like a madwoman."

She laughed and he was relieved she wasn't so afraid that she'd forgotten how to laugh, even if it did sound a little forced. "You should get some rest," she told him. "You're sleeping in my room with Angie."

Gustavo balked at that. "I can't take your room from you," he said with a shake of his head.

She waved his protest away. "It's fine, and I'm sure it would bother Angie if she woke up and I was there instead of you. I'm happy sleeping on the couch. And besides," she confessed, "I don't think I'll be able to sleep for quite a while."

Gustavo didn't think he'd sleep, either, and there was no chance he'd leave her out in the living room alone, listening to every sound of the house and wondering if it were an intruder, which he had no doubt was exactly what would happen. "How about we look at flights for tomorrow?" he suggested. He had a strong desire to comb through the papers they'd taken from the house, see if there was anything important in there, but keeping everyone safe was the most important, and he couldn't be sure they weren't being watched.

That thought made him feel trapped, and for the first time, he actually looked forward to getting away from Colby.

Jeannie agreed and soon they were settled on the couch together. Jeannie pulled her laptop from where it had been tucked beneath the couch and opened it. Gustavo saw what looked like magazine advertisements before she closed them and brought up her browser.

"Were those some of the ads you work on?" he asked, curious.

She shifted her body a little, as if uncomfortable. "Yeah," she told him. "My team sends them to me for review, and even though I'm technically on vacation, I try to take a peek here and there."

"Can I see?" he asked.

Jeannie hesitated, then opened the folder. She showed him a few of the changes she'd made to a recent campaign, and he immediately noticed that she was good at it. And that she hated it. "You don't like this job," he said, a statement more than a question.

She shifted again. "Not really, but it pays well."

He gave a little sigh and she looked at him defensively. "Not everyone needs to like their job, Gustavo," she said.

He nodded. "But you're good at so many things," he said. "And you have so much passion. I hope someday you will do something you truly enjoy."

She looked as if she was about to argue, but he didn't want to have a fight now. Not after all they'd been through today. "Speaking of money, how about we purchase last minute plane tickets for nine people?" he suggested.

She paused for a moment, looking as if she might argue, but then her shoulders relaxed. "Let's do that," she replied. "Where can we go that's snowy?" she asked.

They looked at all the flights leaving the next day. "We could go to Seattle," he suggested. "There's a lot of skiing around there, right?"

Jeannie hesitated. "There is," she said. "Oh how about that one to Denver? I'd like to see Denver."

Gustavo wondered if Jeannie disliked her chosen city as well as her chosen job, but decided to say nothing. They looked at the flight to Denver and, while the cost was painful, it was worth it.

Once he had finally entered the information for each person and paid, they searched for a house to rent for the month, and Gustavo could feel Jeannie

cringing with the expense of it all, but she said nothing and soon everything was done.

Gustavo leaned away from the computer, glad to
be finished. "So it's settled, then. Church, then a
flight and then Colorado for the month."

He was grateful they were staying for church the
next day. He needed a little time with God to process
everything that had happened in so short a time.

"How can you afford all that?" she asked him,
leaning back, too.

"I saved a lot when I was a lawyer," he explained,
"plus my dad left me some in his will. And I'm doing
consulting now, which makes way less than when
I was working full time, but it's enough and it lets
me stay home with Angie. I was hoping I'd get the
ranch making enough money to keep us afloat, but
whatever happens, I know God will be with us and
we'll figure it out somehow."

She nodded, and he wondered if that made her
nervous. Maybe she wouldn't want to be with him
if he wasn't making enough.

He pushed that aside. Of all the things to worry
about, that seemed so minor. He would do whatever
he needed to in order to be with her, and that was
that. Nothing else mattered in comparison.

Without thinking, he reached over and touched
her cheek, and he looked into her beautiful emerald
eyes. There was a long moment where neither of them
spoke.

It was late, but he didn't want to leave her alone

on the couch. And he couldn't imagine being able to get any rest, either. "Should we watch something, or are you too tired?" he asked.

He could see the relief on her face. "I'm not going to sleep any time soon," she said, grabbing the remote. "What should we watch?"

He mulled it over. "Is there something where two attractive people solve a case and everything definitely ends happily with no danger whatsoever?"

Jeannie thought for a second, her lips pursing in that serious way he loved so much. "None that I can think of. Can I interest you in a Christmas movie where a prince falls in love with a commoner and they get everything they wish for despite all the odds against them?"

"Sold," Gustavo responded.

Jeannie beamed. He remembered how much she loved Christmas and all the movies, and it felt wonderful to see her in her holiday mood even with everything else going on. Her entire family had always been excited about the Christmas season, getting the tree up the day after Thanksgiving every year.

The thought made him look around, realizing for the first time what was missing in the living room. "Why don't you have a tree yet?" he asked.

Her eyes dropped to her lap, the mood shifting suddenly, and he realized the reason without her needing to say anything. "Your mom," he said, putting a hand on her arm.

She nodded, her eyes back on the TV. He could

see the sadness there, but it seemed like she wasn't pushing it away as she had before, and for that he was glad. "I know she'd want us to get one, but none of us have brought it up. It's a hard time of the year," she confessed.

Gustavo wished there was something he could do. "I'm here, if there's any way I can help," he told her, hoping she took his offer seriously.

Jeannie turned to him, the spark back in her eyes. "How about we get one as soon as we get settled in Colorado?" she asked.

Gustavo agreed immediately. "We'll get one your mom would go crazy over," he told her, and she smiled.

He couldn't believe it, but he was actually looking forward to the next day. He would spend it with Jeannie, and really, that was all he hoped for in his life. And whatever happened after, they would have the next month together with their families, celebrating Christmas. He felt blessed, despite all that had happened recently.

The two of them settled in to watch the movie. Gustavo put his arm around Jeannie and she curled her body against his, and he felt content.

When Jeannette woke up, it was dark with just the tiniest bit of dawn peeking through the clouds. She had slept with her head resting on Gustavo's chest. She sat up and rubbed her neck, sore from sleeping in such an awkward position. Gustavo was still out;

his head lolled to one side where he had put a pillow at some point after she'd dozed off on him. He had also managed to get a blanket on her, though how he did that with one arm pinned behind her was anybody's guess.

Gustavo stirred and opened his eyes. "How are you doing?" he asked.

"I'm not sure," she said. "Better, I suppose."

She hoped they were safe now, that once they were in Colorado she wouldn't feel as if she was constantly in danger, but it would be a while before she didn't jump at tiny sounds. She still felt antsy, as if she needed to keep moving for some reason. And she felt the need to say goodbye to her childhood home. She wasn't sure if she would ever see it again, or if it would be the same even if she did.

"How about a walk before everyone wakes up?" she proposed.

Gustavo nodded and they put on their boots and jackets and slipped out of the house quietly. The sky was clouded over and the air was damp, and she was sure the rain would start again soon.

They took each other's hands and began their walk around the property. "Anything you want to talk about?" he asked, looking over at her.

"No," she said, squeezing his hand. "I just want to walk."

He seemed to understand, and together they wandered, Jeannette lost in her thoughts about rare books, murder, money, goodbyes and love. She couldn't believe all of this had started just a few days before. It was so much in such a short amount of time.

She didn't pay much attention to where they were walking until Gustavo squeezed her hand. "Hey, we're almost to our fence post," he told her.

She looked up and saw where they were, and her heart felt lighter, remembering a happy, humid summer day when they were sixteen, sitting out in the sun. He'd gotten the idea to carve their names into a post there on the corner of her family's land, making her giggle.

Jeannette began to speak with a little sigh. "I've avoided coming out here since we split. I knew it would be so hard to see that reminder of our best times. But it'll be good to see them now."

Gustavo stopped walking and Jeannette looked at him in confusion. "Jeannie," he said softly, gesturing toward the defaced post.

She strained to see the names, and then her breath caught in her throat. Their names were there, worn from years of weather, but the ugly cuts over each name were very *very* fresh.

And the knife under them hadn't been there before, either.

Jeannie tried to absorb what she was seeing. "He… he…" she stammered, unable to say anything more than that.

"I know," Gustavo said.

She felt like she might faint, and then suddenly

Gustavo was gripping her shoulders and turning her away from the post. "Jeannie, look at me," he told her.

Finally her eyes focused on his. "He was desperate to get us to stop," Gustavo said, his voice hardly registering through her fear. "And we are stopping. He knows that now. He did this before we sent that text yesterday. Now he knows we're leaving and he won't hurt us. He *can't* hurt us."

She heard what he was saying and she hoped he was right. She worried she wouldn't be strong enough to make it through her fear.

"Will you pray with me?" he asked.

It was the perfect thing for them to do at that moment. Her hands were trembling, but she took his in her own and leaned against him, closing her eyes.

"Lord, keep us safe," he began. "We trust in You and have faith in You."

Jeannette could feel her body calming, her pulse returning to normal. She squeezed his hands tighter.

"And thank You," he said. "I have missed this woman so much, and to have her in my life is an answer to my prayers"

Jeannette felt tears stinging her eyes, knowing that he could feel that level of gratitude even during terrible moments like this.

He continued, "Please help us through this journey, Lord. Amen."

"Amen," Jeannette repeated.

When they opened their eyes, Gustavo leaned

down and pressed a soft kiss against her lips, making her heart flutter.

"I love you, Jeannette Marie Lawson. I have since middle school and I won't ever stop. I will carve our name on every fence post I can find for the rest of our lives, and create thousands of wonderful new memories with you. We will move past this and have a great life together," he assured her.

Jeannette had no words, so she leaned forward and kissed him again, then pressed her forehead against his. He held her hands tight, and it felt right and good, and she thanked God for it. Her fears and worries melted in the presence of Gustavo's faith and optimism.

"I love you, too," she whispered, feeling tears in her eyes.

As they began the walk to the house together, she felt hope bubbling inside her. They would leave this awful place and start a life together somewhere else, somewhere safe.

But as she looked at the house she grew up in, she hated that she would need to say goodbye to her home. This would always be her home, she realized, and a part of her would always live in Colby, but now that she needed to leave, she desperately wanted to stay. She vowed to make these last few hours in her hometown good ones.

They reached the porch and she took a final deep breath of the clean air and went inside, where she could hear the first sounds of people stirring.

\* \* \*

Gustavo watched Jeannie carefully, but she seemed calmer. She was, perhaps, a little sad, but resolved and holding his hand tightly, and he believed everything would be okay.

"Papa!" he heard, along with a knock on a distant door. "Angie's awake," he told Jeannie. He hated letting go of her hand, but she gave him a little wave and wandered off, so he turned and rushed to the room and opened the door, where the little girl stood with bright eyes, well rested and happy. It seemed like the events of the night before and sleeping in a strange place had left her none the worse for wear, and she climbed into his outstretched arms, ready for her day.

Beth walked up behind them, a pile of clothes in her hands. "These should fit Angie. Feel free to keep whatever you like. They aren't going to any use in those tubs."

Gustavo thanked her and took the clothes, and soon Angie was decked out in a sparkly unicorn shirt and superhero pants, ready for church. Gustavo had felt embarrassed the first time he took his toddler to service in the crazy clothes she chose after he'd given up attempting to convince her to wear a nice dress, but he'd quickly realized that nobody who had a toddler expected anything different, and from then on he let her choose for herself without a fight.

At breakfast, everyone complimented her on her look and Angie beamed with all the attention. Gustavo had never considered that Angie might get lonely with just him, but seeing how she reacted to this big caring family, his heart felt tight in his chest. He wanted her to have that in her life, and he was glad she'd have it for at least the next month—hopefully forever, if Jeannie wanted that, too.

"How are you this morning, Mama?" he asked his mother as she entered the room, looking tidy and ready for the day.

She sat to eat, thanking Mr. Lawson for the bedroom and the meal. "I am wonderful, *gracias*, *mijo*," she said. "Did you find flights?"

"We're going to Colorado. I booked us a big house for the month right near a ski resort," he said.

The adults all seemed satisfied with this, the children ecstatic. "We're going to ski!" Carson shouted, and the others added their voices to the mix, each one discussing the various activities they would participate in while on vacation in the mountains.

Mr. Lawson looked over at Gustavo. "Do you need something to wear today?" he asked, noticing that Gustavo was still in the same clothes from yesterday.

Gustavo shook his head. "I have a bag in the truck. I'll run and grab it."

Mr. Lawson nodded. "Good. Then you can use the shower in my room. I think the other will be a little crowded this morning."

Gustavo jogged out to the truck in the soft morning light, trying to avoid the puddles as best he could. He was happy that the rain was still holding off, and even though he could see clouds on the horizon, he couldn't help but feel hopeful, though he purposely kept his eyes away from the corner of the field that held the defaced fence post.

He opened the duffel and the first thing he saw was the angel ornament. He touched it gently, thinking of Jeannie holding it out to him, and then he pulled out some clothes, set the angel on top of the rest and went inside. Mr. Lawson was standing there by the door, and Gustavo followed him to the older man's bedroom.

As Mr. Lawson walked him through to the bathroom door, Gustavo looked around the room. Suncatchers hung on every window, and he imagined the room would be filled with colored light on bright days. "How are you doing?" Gustavo asked.

Mr. Lawson gave a sad shrug. "I miss Ellie every day, but I see her in our daughters and grandchildren, and I know she'll be there waiting for me when it's my time," he said.

Gustavo could hear the grief beneath the words and his heart ached for the man. "I'm grateful for the time I had with her," Mr. Lawson added. "You don't want to miss out on any more time to be with the woman you love," he finished.

Gustavo nodded, understanding what Jeannie's father was telling him. He would do everything in his power to spend as much time as he could with the woman he loved, if she would let him.

Mr. Lawson patted him on the shoulder. "Go

get showered and changed so we aren't late," he prompted and left. Gustavo watched the man go with his own mind whirring.

He and Jeannie still had a connection, that much was obvious. And he loved her. But would he be enough? He would do what he needed to do, he decided. As long as it didn't harm Angie—she came above everything, even his own happiness—he would do anything to have Jeannie stay in his life.

When he was washed and dressed, he went in search for his daughter and found her playing with Jeannie in the living room. They were seated on the floor facing each other, playing a clapping game that Jeannie was trying to teach the little girl. Squishy Papa was on the floor between them.

He watched the two of them, his heart swelling. He wasn't the only one who needed Jeannie in his life. Angie needed her, too. It was easy to see that the girl loved her already.

Jeannie looked up at him and grinned, and his heart thumped painfully in his chest. "Come on, everybody, we're going to be late!" Beth called, breaking the moment with her orders. "And it might rain again so I expect everyone to be in boots," she added.

Her three kids ripped through the room toward the front door, a storm of shouts and boots and coats, Beth following calmly behind. "Let's get going, you three," she said with a shooing gesture as she walked through the living room, and Jeannie and Angie stood.

When Beth spoke, there was no room for argument, so they got their boots and jackets on—Beth had spare boots and a raincoat for Angie—and they all walked out into the cool morning. Gustavo followed the rest of the family out the door.

"Can I ride with you?" Beth asked, walking over to Gustavo's truck and giving him pleading eyes. "These kids have been a little much this morning and I could use the relative quiet."

Gustavo looked over at his mother. "Would you be willing to ride with Mr. Lawson, Mama?" he asked.

His mother laughed as she watched the mayhem. "*Sí*, you go on, Beth," she said as if she was one of the family.

Gustavo turned to Beth. "Then you certainly can."

"But *may* she?" Jeannie called out sarcastically as she climbed into the rear with Angie and adjusted the things they'd gathered from Gustavo's house so there would be enough room to sit.

Beth smiled. "It didn't take you two very long to get into a groove, did it?" she asked Gustavo quietly.

He grinned. "Old habits die hard, I guess."

"She's different with you around, you know. Happier and feisty. It's good for her, even with all this mess going on," Beth said, moving around to the passenger side before he could respond. "Jeannette Marie, what are you doing in the backseat? I can sit there."

"Angie and I are having a good time together.

You sit up there and talk to an adult for a change," Jeannie responded.

Gustavo chuckled at the sisterly bickering as he settled into his seat. He wondered if what Beth said was true. He hoped he brought the best out in Jeannie. He knew she did that to him and he wanted to repay the favor.

Before they started driving, though, he took a glance at Jeannie in the rearview mirror and saw the expression on her face. He could tell she was reliving the night before, feeling everything from the past two days over again, and he turned in his seat to face her. "You okay?" he asked seriously. "If you'd rather we don't go—"

"I want to go to church," Jeannie said firmly, buckling her seat belt. "It'll be fine."

He nodded, turned around and started the truck. They followed Mr. Lawson's white SUV, and Gustavo could hear the two in the back talking to each other. Jeannie seemed less tense, and he hoped that once they were in Colorado she could be her happy self without all the tension and fear of the last few days.

Beth gave a big sigh. "Thank you. If I had to hear one more argument about who has the best superpower this morning, I'd be going to church to pray for a whole lot of forgiveness. And with a flight this afternoon, getting away from them for a few minutes was very necessary."

"It must be a lot to do it all on your own," Gustavo said to her, "but it seems like you're doing an amazing job."

Beth gave him a grateful look. "I have a lot of help, with Dad and Jeannie around. And it'll be easier when David gets back," she said.

Gustavo didn't think he'd ever met Beth's husband, but he had heard the kids talking about him at dinner. "He's on an aircraft carrier right now?"

Beth nodded. "He'll return mid-January. I'm sorry he'll miss Christmas, but we'll celebrate all the holidays he's missed when he gets back. It will be wonderful to see him in person instead of on a screen," she said.

Gustavo could hear the love in her voice and he envied her, even though her spouse was who knew how many miles away. She seemed happy, content. Full of faith that soon the difficult times would be at an end and she would have her family complete again.

The church was close to downtown, and the short drive went by without incident. Gustavo felt relieved. He had to hope it was all over and they were safe now. He opened the door to the backseat so he could unbuckle Angie from her car seat, but Jeannie was undoing the last clasp when he did, and Angie practically hopped into his arms. He squeezed her tight while Jeannie and Beth got out from the other side, and soon they were standing together, watching Mr. Lawson, his mom and Beth's children climb out of the other car. The oldest two were saying something about speed versus flight and Gustavo tried not to chuckle as Beth groaned. His mom gave him a bright smile and he thought perhaps a month with this family would do her some good, too.

They dropped the children off in their respective Sunday school rooms—Gustavo was shocked when Angie ran right into the room holding her Squishy Papa without any protest, and needed to reassure himself that she'd be safe without him—and then the adults entered the main service.

Gustavo took a few deep breaths and allowed his mind to calm, though he still felt worried. Angie not being in his sight terrified him, but he reminded himself that it would be okay and tried to turn his attention to the service. It was a message of faith and hope, and he listened, feeling the importance of the words. It was an opportunity to feel God's love and assurance that everything would be okay.

He looked over, saw the fear on Jeannie's face and whispered to her, "Everything is okay. We're all safe here."

She visibly relaxed and he tried to get his mind back on the pastor. There was a strange feeling, though, a thought he couldn't entirely ignore: what if Anthony—a murderer—was there, sitting in this congregation with them and watching them? Gustavo looked around carefully, seeing many familiar faces but not that one.

With God's help, Anthony would keep their families out of danger. He took another calming breath and listened to the sound of voices as everyone began to sing a hymn.

When the service was over, he went to get Angie, who flew into his arms and began telling him about all the adventures she'd had over the past hour. Relief flowed through him once he was sure everybody was safe, and he told himself that they were going to make it through this okay. They would be on their flight in a matter of hours. He listened to Angie's chatter, letting it carry them out of the building and into the parking lot. The sky was clear and sunny, and he hoped it was a good omen.

That's when he noticed that Angie's hands were empty. "Where's Squishy Papa?" he asked.

Angie's expression turned from joy to dismay as she realized she wasn't holding her doll, and it seemed like her expression was about to turn to utter devastation. "I'll go get it, Angie," Jeannie told the little girl, putting a hand on her arm. "You stay with real Papa and I'll meet you at the car with Squishy Papa. Can you be brave while I do that?"

Angie nodded, visibly upset but not wailing, and Jeannie turned and ran back into the building before Gustavo could even thank her.

The rest of the family stood nearby, waiting. "We don't have long before we need to leave for the airport," Gustavo's mother said, "and I must pack. The children and Mr. Lawson and I will leave, *si*?"

Mr. Lawson agreed and they started walking toward his car. "I think I'll squeeze in with them,"

Beth said, looking anxious. "I need to pack for four people."

Gustavo waved as she dashed after the rest of the group, and suddenly he and Angie were waiting for Jeannie alone.

He hugged Angie tight and walked toward his truck, reminding her that Jeannie would be back very soon with the precious object. He was so focused on calming the girl in his arms that he didn't notice the folded piece of paper under his windshield until he was standing beside the hood. Wondering what it could be, he pulled the paper off and unfolded it.

*I'll be watching.*

Gustavo looked around, feeling adrenaline course through him, making his skin itch for action. He looked for Anthony, but didn't see him anywhere, then scanned the top of the church, hoping for a camera, but there were none that he could see.

He noticed Jeannie coming closer, a genuine smile on her face, holding Squishy Papa. She looked like normal happy Jeannie, not the scared version he'd seen so many times the past few days.

Gustavo stuffed the note into his back pocket.

"Here you are!" Jeannie declared, proudly handing the doll to the excited girl, who grabbed it and hugged it tightly to her chest. Then she turned to Gustavo. "Did everybody else leave?"

He nodded. "They wanted to start packing. You should pack, too."

"What about you?" she asked.

He had thought about that. "I have the things in my duffel, including plenty of things for Angie from your sister. I don't think I'll go back to that house," he said.

He hated how permanent those words felt, but there didn't seem to be any other choice.

"I guess we should go pack up like everybody else," she said, giving him a little smile that seemed to say everything was better; they were safe now.

He couldn't tell her about the note. He didn't want her living her life in fear. So he got Angie in her car seat and they settled in to drive to Jeannie's childhood home, maybe for the last time.

# Chapter Nine

Jeannette looked over at Gustavo, who seemed on edge. She didn't blame him. So much had happened that she doubted she would feel normal again for a very long time.

But perhaps in a new city, far away from what had happened here, they could begin to feel normal again. And they would be together, which made her optimistic.

Still, she was sad to say goodbye. And in some cases, just disappear without saying anything. Guilt roiled inside her and she made a quick decision. "Gustavo," she said, turning toward him. "I want to go tell Linda and Henry I'm leaving. I can't go without telling Henry I'm leaving."

Gustavo looked uncertain for a moment, but then he nodded and turned the truck toward downtown. Jeannette smiled at him. "Thank you," she said.

He nodded, but seemed preoccupied. "Is there

something wrong?" she asked. "Something new, I mean," she added, realizing how ridiculous that sounded. There had been so many things wrong it was hard to keep track.

He seemed to hesitate for a moment. "I'm ready to be done with this," he said at last, sounding care-worn.

Her heart went out to him. She put a hand on his shoulder. "I'll talk to Henry for two minutes and then we'll pack and get out of this town. Christmas in Colorado will be wonderful," she said.

He parked near Linda's store and pulled Jeannette in for a hug, their seat belts pulling at them.

"Should I run in and you wait here?" she asked, but Gustavo was shaking his head before she even finished speaking. "I'd like us to all stay together," he said.

So they got out of the car and Jeannette knocked loudly on the glass door so Linda would hear even if she was in the back room.

After a few minutes, Linda walked up to the door, looking harried. Jeannette tried to smile to show she was okay, even though it wasn't actually true. She *wasn't* okay, but she would be. Linda opened the door a little. "I'm not open yet, Jeannie," she said, sounding a little stern.

"I know, I'm sorry to drop in like this, but we're leaving for the airport in a couple of hours and I couldn't leave without saying goodbye to Henry," she told the older woman.

Linda's face softened. "You're leaving?" she asked.

Jeannette nodded. "It's for the best. We ran into a bit of trouble and we're going to go on a little vacation through Christmas."

Linda glanced at Gustavo, but didn't say anything. Jeannette knew she couldn't explain right now, but she'd send an e-mail another time—though she wouldn't tell the woman about the murder or the threats. She didn't want to put her friend in danger.

"Can we come in and say goodbye? We'll just be here for a minute. I promise. I know how hurt Henry is if people don't say goodbye," Jeannette said.

Linda opened the door and let them in. Jeannette started walking quickly through the dark store and toward the back, where Henry would be. He had his own little area, and Linda lived above the store. She'd been there enough times as a teenager to lead the way, and her sense of urgency told her they needed to get in and get out.

In case Anthony thought they were breaking the rules.

Gustavo followed close behind her with Angie chattering in his arms and Linda brought up the rear. She seemed like she was trying to say something, but Jeannette felt so rushed she hardly noticed. She walked through the open EMPLOYEES ONLY door and straight through the little living area there, barely noticing the old couch where she had sat so many times, drinking tea and chatting with Linda.

It was sad that she wouldn't have the chance to

do that again, that she could only spare it a glance as she passed through.

When she got to Henry's door, it was open and she could see the large man sitting on a chair, looking at tiny pretty things. She knocked on the door and he looked up. His face split into a wide grin. "Jean-Jean!" he shouted, coming over to hug her.

Jeannette hugged him tightly and felt tears in her eyes. "Hi, Henry. I wanted to come by and say I'm sorry I couldn't visit yesterday," she told him.

"Can you visit now?" he said, sounding excited. "I can show you my collection."

He grabbed her hand and led her over to the items on the table. "I wish I could, Henry, but I'm about to go. I—"

That was when Jeannette noticed the small silver and blue pendant on the table. She dug into her pocket and pulled out the little glass bead they had found in Ricky Gibraltar's house.

It matched.


Gustavo stood near the couch, where he could see Jeannie as she talked to Henry, but far enough away to give her a little privacy.

"I wasn't expecting guests," Linda said, clearing off the little table in a rush, looking frazzled.

"Don't worry, we'll be gone soon," Gustavo assured her.

He felt bad to be imposing and grabbed the little wastebasket that stood near the couch, holding it out to her so she could put the papers she'd gathered into it. She looked nervous, as if she wasn't sure what to do, and then his glance landed on the papers in her hands. She tried to cover them with her arms, but it was too late. It was the same handwriting—the same heavy black marker.

They matched the one he'd found on his car.

He looked at her, mouth open, and she dropped the papers in panic. "Did you write that note?" he asked, looking at the other pages, other threats and notes, as if she'd made several different versions.

She didn't answer, but the truth of it was right there in front of him. "Why?" he asked.

"Because she killed Ricky Gibraltar," Jeannie said, stepping out of Henry's room with something clenched in her hand, closing the door behind her.

Linda looked at Jeannie, then Gustavo. "You shouldn't be here," she said, her voice a whimper.

"I don't know how I didn't think of it," Jeannie said, sounding angry, as she stepped closer to the old woman. "I couldn't figure out how a couple of kids got rid of rare books without getting caught, but of course that wouldn't be hard for you, with all the connections you had through the store. You used him and then you murdered him," Jeannie finished.

Linda crumpled into the chair, suddenly looking every bit her age and more. "It wasn't the way you think," she said. "Ricky and I came up with the idea together after he applied for a job here. We both needed money and we were going to split it down the middle. Henry needed special classes, and if I didn't find the money somehow, I would lose the store," she said, her voice pleading.

Gustavo turned and set Angie on the floor, hoping Linda didn't notice as he slowly extricated his phone and quickly swiped a message. Then he stood, hid Angie behind his legs and hoped she would stay there.

Neither woman was looking at him. Linda was looking desperately at Jeannie, and Jeannie was showing that her fear had turned to white-hot anger.

He watched, wishing he could do something to help, but knowing he needed to stay there and protect his little girl.

Jeannette felt angry and shocked and betrayed by this person she had called a friend. "You threatened me. You murdered Ricky," she said, pointing an accusatory finger at Linda.

"I had no choice!" Linda shouted back. "He was going to turn himself in! He wanted to give back all the books. I couldn't let him do that. And I couldn't let you find out and tell people now, after so long. I can't leave Henry all on his own. You have to understand."

Jeannette's heart broke thinking about the sweet man sitting in his room only a few feet away. He was so dependent on his mother, but she held herself firm. "That's not an excuse to steal and murder,

Linda, and you know it. You need to give yourself up to the police."

"No!" Linda cried out, her voice strangled with fear. "Henry needs me. You know that! Jeannie, how could you want this for me? For him?"

"I'll do everything I can to make sure he's taken care of," Jeannette promised, trying to calm herself as much as she could, though she was shaking all over. She looked over at Gustavo and took strength from his presence. He gave her a little nod of support and she turned her attention to Linda. "But you committed crimes, including murder."

Linda shook her head. "I didn't mean to," she said.

Jeannette raised her eyebrows, not convinced by the older woman. "You came into his room and killed him in the middle of the night, but you didn't mean to do it? I don't believe that, Linda."

Linda stood, her eyes flashing, and she stormed away from both Jeannette and Gustavo. Jeannette was about to chase after her when Linda returned, but this time with an ugly black gun in her hand. She pointed the gun at Jeannette's heart, and Jeannette felt her legs go weak.

When Linda spoke, her voice was full of frustration and fear. "I warned you, Jeannie! I knew you would keep pushing and searching until you found some answers, so I worked very hard to make sure you'd understand the consequences if you did, but you couldn't just let it go, that you should leave if you wanted to stay safe. I thought the house and the car and the texts and the fence would be enough, but you came here anyway. Why wouldn't you just listen?"

Jeannette felt panic threatening to overwhelm her, but she did her best to keep it controlled. All her anger dropped away at the sight of that gun.

She silently asked God to keep her safe and spoke in the calmest voice she could manage. "That's one thing I really don't understand. How did you send the anonymous texts?" she asked, stalling for time.

Linda rolled her eyes. "I'm old, but I'm not stupid. I did an internet search and found an app."

"The police will be able to trace those messages, Linda," Gustavo said, his voice low, calm. He took a step or two toward Jeannette, who watched in terror and wondered where Angie was.

Linda looked shaken, turning her attention to him. "No, they were anonymous. I signed up with a fake e-mail and everything," she said.

Jeannette wanted desperately to get her attention away from Gustavo, back on herself, but Linda only had eyes for him as he shook his head slowly.

"If you used an app, it's downloaded onto your phone," he told her. "The police will know, and all this will come out no matter what happens to us. You need to turn yourself in. That's your only choice now."

Jeannette saw Linda's hand shaking and could feel panic rise in her chest. She couldn't let Gustavo or Angie get hurt. "Don't do this, Linda," Jeannette said loudly, and Linda whipped her head toward her.

Words gushed out of her, though she hardly knew what she was saying. "It's too late. Set down the gun. People know we're here. Hurting us will only make it worse."

Jeannette wished what she said was true, but she knew she hadn't told anybody where they were going. What if Linda murdered them and nobody ever found out?

Linda's eyes were wilder than ever, her fear and anger giving her the look of a cornered animal. "If that's all true then my life's over anyway, and you deserve to feel some of the pain you've caused me. You ruined everything," she said, taking aim at Jeannette's chest.

Jeannette stood there, frozen, watching the barrel of the gun and realizing that there was nothing she could do to stop it from happening. She thought of her family, and of Gustavo and Angie, and a tear slipped down her cheek as she waited for the pain to come.

"No!" Gustavo shouted, his voice echoing loudly in the small space, and he moved quickly toward Linda.

Linda shifted her attention—and the gun—toward him. Jeannette could see that if Linda was fast enough, she would shoot Gustavo before he could do anything to stop her.

Without thinking, Jeannette flung herself at Linda, throwing her body against the older woman's. They both tumbled to the floor, Jeannette's head smacking against the concrete floor hard enough to make everything go gray. The gun went off, loud and echoing, but Jeannette hardly noticed through the fog.

She lay there, breathing hard, her vision going in and out, her hearing muffled. She thought she might vomit. There were movements and sounds, but she couldn't focus on anything that was happening around her.

Jeannette had no idea how long she lay there, panting, but at some point, two arms wrapped tight around her and pulled her close to a warm body. "Jeannie," Gustavo said, his warm voice rumbling through her. "Stay with me, Jeannie."

"She confessed," Jeannette told him. "It was her. Is Angie…?"

Then everything went black.

# Chapter Ten

When Jeannette opened her eyes again, she was in a beige, brightly-lit room, lying in a bed, and Linda was nowhere to be seen. Only Gustavo was the same, sitting and watching her with a relieved smile. "What happened?" she asked, trying to sit up only to feel pain rush through her.

Gustavo put a hand on her arm. "Rest, Jeannie. The doctors said you'll be fine, but you need to rest."

"Did I get shot?" Jeannette asked, scanning her body for points of pain, but it all seemed to be centered in her head.

Gustavo shook his head. "No, the gun went off when Linda fell, but it didn't hit anyone. You banged your head hard enough on the floor to give you a concussion, though."

Jeannette went through the events she could remember. "You could've been hurt, Gustavo," she said, looking at him with love. Then she realized who else had been there. "And Angie. Is Angie okay?" she said to him with a gasp, looking around for the little girl.

He nodded. "Angie is fine. I'm fine. We're all okay. My mom has her right now."

"Gustavo, I'm so sorry," she said, tears overflowing. "I put both of you in danger."

"You didn't know, Jeannie, and neither did I. But now we're all safe. Linda is in custody. The police came in after you fell and they arrested her. You did a wonderful job, Jeannie."

"I could have gotten us killed," she said, unable to deny the waves of guilt.

Gustavo got out of his chair and squeezed his body onto the little hospital bed with her, wrapping his arm carefully around her. She let the warmth of him engulf her.

"When I saw that gun pointed at you," he said, kissing her cheek, "I thought I was going to lose the love of my life after I'd just found her again. I am so thankful you're alive."

She couldn't let herself off that easily, even if he could. "It was all my fault in the first place, telling her exactly how to steal those books," she said.

He wiped the tears from her face with a sweep of his thumb. "This wasn't your fault," he told her, his voice emphatic. "You shared an observation. That was all. It wasn't Ricky's fault either. A child is not responsible for what a grown woman did. You were so brave today, and you kept us all safe."

"How?" she asked.

"You kept her distracted long enough for me to contact the police, and now she can't hurt us or our families," he told her.

Jeannette tried to absorb his words, but she was still shaken and racked with guilt. She wasn't sure what to say.

"And," he added, "the police found a little snow globe among Henry's other treasures. One with a Christmas tree in the middle, just like Mr. Gibraltar described. He's agreed to give it back to Mr. Gibraltar, along with the pendant. When Linda confessed, she said that Henry had loved Ricky's necklace, and when it broke, she took that piece to give to him. She'd been the one to clear out Ricky's old room after he died, taking any evidence with her she could find, except that one book Ricky had hidden," he finished.

"Until Angie found it," Jeannette added. "What will happen to Henry?" she asked, thinking of the sweet man who would be so affected by his mother's choices.

"Mrs. Shelley has promised to take care of him," Gustavo told her, sending a wave of relief through her. "It seems like she's been pretty lonely since her husband died, and she'd spent nearly every day with him at CuriosCity, so he seems happy with the arrangement."

Jeannette tried to smile, but it hurt and she stopped, resting her head against Gustavo instead. She felt so tired she could hardly move. Gustavo gave her a tiny squeeze, and for the first time since they started all of this, she felt truly safe.

At that moment there was a little knock on the door that made her jump, causing pain to radiate from behind her eyes again, and she wondered how long it would be before she would relax completely. She snuggled deeper into his embrace and watched the door, wondering who it could be.

It opened, and Anthony Pinker was standing there with flowers. "Hi," he said softly, sounding a little shy. "I hope it's okay that I'm here."

Jeannette waved him in, feeling embarrassed that she'd wrongly suspected him of the thefts. She decided to start fresh and know him as an adult, rather than write him off for his behavior as a teenager. After all, they had all been foolish teenagers once, she thought, holding tight to Gustavo.

"I came to apologize and to thank you," Anthony said.

Jeannette wasn't sure she'd heard him correctly. "Thank me? Why?" she asked, confused.

"I told you not to dig into the case when you brought in the book because I didn't want you to look into Ricky Gibraltar and discover he was the thief. He was a good kid, but I knew he was making some bad decisions," he explained. "He even borrowed my ID a couple of times. He told me it was because I was eighteen already and he wanted to buy cigarettes, but now I know it was to help him not get caught if the book thefts were ever discovered."

It seemed like Anthony had been waiting nearly two decades to tell his story, and he sat and continued without pause, keeping his eyes on the flowers. "He'd been behaving strangely, and I knew something was wrong. I tried to get him to tell me about it the evening he fell in that mine shaft. He got so upset when I confronted him that he'd tried to run away and slipped and fell. But I didn't know anybody else was involved, or that he was murdered that night. If it wasn't for you, I would have always believed he died from that fall and that it was my fault, so thank you for clearing my conscience about that."

Jeannette tried to feel good about that, but her chagrin for being wrong about his involvement made it difficult.

"And I thought you'd like to know," Anthony continued, "Linda has agreed to cooperate and help us find the stolen originals. We'll finally get them back to the library, God willing."

Jeannette wished she had words to say, a way to thank Anthony and to apologize, but her head throbbed and her whole body felt so sore and exhausted it was difficult to think. Fortunately, Anthony didn't seem to need a response. He simply set the flowers on the table, gave a little wave and left.

Gustavo kissed Jeannette on the forehead again and she closed her eyes tight. She focused on his arms around her. "How long do I need to stay in the hospital?" she asked, trying to get her mind moving forward.

"Well, they were worried about swelling and your concussion, but it seems like all the tests are in and you're going to be fine. So mostly we've been waiting for you to get back to normal before I took you home."

She could hear the smile in his voice and looked up at him apprehensively. "What do you mean, 'get back to normal'?"

"You had a concussion," he said, failing at hiding his amusement. "So you were saying a lot of nonsense. But you seem fine now," he added.

"What was I saying?" she asked, wondering what she could have said in that state that made him so happy and yet so reluctant to share.

"Well, you kept talking about auburn herrings," he told her, unable to suppress the laughter.

She had absolutely no idea what he was talking about. "Auburn what now?"

"Auburn herrings. Instead of red herrings. You said that the renter Linda told you about was an auburn herring, and Anthony was an auburn herring. You repeated those several times."

Jeannette shook her head. "You're kidding me," she said.

He seemed delighted. "Not at all. It was so funny. You also sang 'Home on the Range' a few times and tried to tell me all about the Big Dark, but it got a bit lost in translation so I'm still not entirely sure what that is."

"It's a Seattle thing," she said with a groan. "When it gets dark and rainy for the entire winter."

Gustavo grimaced a little and Jeannette realized she wasn't exactly selling Washington to him, but then he kissed her on the forehead. "I'm sure we'll manage just fine. Angie loves stomping in puddles."

Jeannette thought about bringing that bright little girl to the city, away from the open fields and her father's ranch. "There are lots of great places to hike," she said, trying to convince them both that they would be happy there.

He held her close and neither of them said anything for a long while.

Finally, Gustavo broke the silence. "Before Angie and I move across the country, though, there's something you and I need to discuss," he said in a quiet, somber voice.

Jeannette turned to him, concerned. She didn't know what had him so worried they would need to "discuss" it, and the not knowing made her nervous. She waited, hoping it wasn't anything too serious.

"Before we leave Colby," he began, sending her brain into a flurry of activity trying to solve the rest of the sentence, "will you marry me, here, in our home town?"

Whatever Jeannette had thought he was about to say, it certainly wasn't that. She stared at him in shocked silence as he pulled a small box from his pocket.

"I know this probably isn't the best moment to ask

you," he said after there was no response for several seconds. "But I wanted to ask as soon as we were safe—here or in Colorado. I would have done it a few hours ago, but I didn't think I could trust you to give an actual answer while you were giggling about herrings. I love you, Jeannette Marie Lawson. I have for as far back as I can remember. I want to be your family and your home, wherever we are."

Jeannette finally convinced herself that this was really happening and squeezed him tightly, feeling tears wet her cheeks. "Yes, of course I'll marry you," she managed to choke out.

She had finally found where she belonged, here in Gustavo's arms, and she wanted to stay there forever.

Gustavo opened the box and Jeannie gasped. "My mom's ring," she said in a breathless whisper.

He nodded. "When I talked to your dad about wanting to propose to you, he offered it," he told her.

Jeannie felt those emotions flow over her, and this time she let them come without a fight. "I miss her so much," she told him through her tears.

"I know," he said, holding her as she cried.

## Chapter Eleven

Christmas morning wasn't exactly as Gustavo had hoped; it was even better. Angie woke up ecstatic, and he followed as she ran out into the living room to see what was left under the tree, which was now covered in ornaments, including the little angel that sparkled so prettily. Angie squealed in delight at everything, from the crayons in her stocking to the wide variety of books and stuffed animals. It did his heart good to see her so happy, and he prayed she would be just as happy up in Seattle.

She would love it, he assured himself, looking around at all the things he would need to pack before the big move. Jeannette had managed to get another two weeks off work, so they had a little time, but he was disappointed that he would never have the chance to fix up this old place like he'd dreamed. Now that they were safe, it felt like home again. Still, he didn't regret his decision. The past few weeks with Jeannie had been like a dream, and he couldn't imagine their life without her in it.

Wherever they were, they would be a family, and that was the important thing. For the past month, they had truly felt like a family—even though Beth's kids had been very disappointed about no longer going to Colorado for a month—and Gustavo was already excited about next Christmas, when Jeannie would be with him in the morning, relaxing in his arms as they watched Angie play. He couldn't wait.

He tried to stay in the moment, but he also looked forward to the time when all the paper was torn and Angie had settled down enough to have breakfast. When she finally sat to eat, he rushed to get dressed, putting on a nice suit for the first time in months. It would have been a little uncomfortable if he wasn't in such a wonderful mood.

After Angie had finished, he said, "It's time to go to Jeannie's and then church," and she hopped up in excitement.

"More presents?" she shouted.

He patted her head. "There might be more presents over there—we'll need to see," he said, which sent her into a flurry of activity as she prepared to leave.

She began gathering as many of her new things as she could to take with her. Gustavo considered limiting her to just a few things, but then he shrugged and grabbed a big empty box and started piling everything into it.

It was Christmas, after all.

On top of everything else, he added the fluffy red Christmas dress he'd gotten for her. It seemed best to wait until the last minute to put it on her to avoid the hundreds of possible ways she could stain it before they left for church, and he was glad of his decision as she stomped through every available puddle on her way to the truck.

In his state of distracted excitement, the drive flew by, and he was at the Lawson house before he knew it. When they arrived, Jeannie came bounding out to meet them as soon as he pulled into the driveway and his heart lifted as he saw her. She was beautiful in snowflake pajama pants and a white top, her hair tied in a ponytail, and she seemed as excited about the day as he was.

It was a cool morning, but she'd run out of the house without a jacket and had her arms hugged around her body to keep herself warm. He watched her, feeling as if she was a gift from God—the perfect match he had known and loved as far back as he could remember.

"Merry Christmas," she said, wrapping her arms around him as soon as he stepped out of the vehicle and shivering against him. "Are you ready for today?"

He smiled, his heart full to bursting, and hugged her close, giving her his warmth. "I'm ready," he said, kissing her forehead.

After a moment, they untangled. He grabbed the

box of toys while she unbuckled Angie and, in short order, all three of them were inside the warm house.

He greeted Mr. Lawson and Beth and the children, who were all gathered around the tree, the floor a mess of wrapping paper and packaging. Beba was there, too, with another small pile of gifts for Angie. The girl wriggled out of Jeannie's arms and ran to open them, and Jeannie and Gustavo joined Beth where she stood, sipped coffee and relaxed on the outskirts of the chaos.

"We should start getting ready soon, or we'll be late getting to the church," Beth said after a few minutes.

Gustavo looked at Jeannette. "Is that what you'll be wearing? Because I love it," he said.

She showed off her pj's with a little flourish. "It is pretty elegant," she said, as if she was considering a change in her wardrobe plan.

He laughed and pulled her closer to him, thanking God for her over and over.

"Before any of that," Mr. Lawson said, "I have a few last gifts to give my daughters."

"Ooh, the secrets of the workshop will finally be revealed," Beth said to Jeannie, looking as excited as Angie had that morning.

Their father waved at them to follow, and soon they were standing in his bedroom, Gustavo following the two women into the small room. In the corner stood a new piece of furniture, a large cabinet made of beautiful dark wood with brightly colored glass gracing the front doors, the sides etched with designs. A large red bow stood proudly on top. The cabinet was a beautiful piece of craftsmanship, and Gustavo imagined it took many hours to complete. When Jeannie and Beth saw it, they both made little noises of excitement.

"This one is for Jeannette," Mr. Lawson said, and she walked over to it, running her hands delicately on the glass inlaid in the doors, and Gustavo realized what they were.

"Mom's suncatchers," she said in a soft whisper, sounding close to tears. She pulled the doors open to reveal shelves inside.

Her father said, "I wanted to give you something that would remind you of her. Your mom always knew how important books were to you and I think she would be happy to know you had something nice to store them in. She always hoped someday you would write your own, and if you ever do, I would be honored if you put them in something I built. But whatever you decide to put in there will make me a proud father."

Jeannie looked at her dad and Gustavo could see the joy and sadness mingled in her eyes. He knew how much this meant to her and he hoped Mr. Lawson did, too. From the way his eyes sparkled, Gustavo was pretty sure he understood. Jeannie hugged her father, and when she broke away, both of their faces were wet with tears.

"I'm not sure how we'll get it to Seattle safely," Mr. Lawson said, "But we'll figure it out."

"Actually," Jeannie said, looking at Gustavo. "I think it should stay in Colby."

Gustavo wrinkled his eyebrows, not sure what she meant. "You don't want to take it with us?" he asked.

Jeannie shook her head. "I don't want us to go, either. I want this bookshelf at the ranch, where we belong."

Gustavo gaped at her. "But what about Seattle? And your job?"

"I quit," she said, giving him the biggest grin. "I didn't like my job, and I don't want to live in Seattle. I'm going to try my hand at writing books like I've always wanted, and if that doesn't work, there's always a job for me at the library," she said with a smile. "I hope it's okay I didn't tell you, but I wanted to surprise you."

He laughed, his heart full to bursting. "Are you sure this is what you want?" he asked.

Jeannie nodded seriously. "I've been thinking about this for weeks and this is our home. We don't need a lot of money to be happy. I want to be here, with our families."

Gustavo hugged her tight, the life before him more wonderful than he could have ever dreamed.

"I'm so glad you're coming home," Beth said to her sister. Then she looked around. "But more importantly, where's my present? Am I getting a bookshelf, too?" she asked, seeming more than a little disappointed that there was nothing in that room for her.

Her father smiled mischievously. "Your gift is in the living room," he said, attempting to sound nonchalant.

Beth looked confused. "We were just in the living room," she said, sounding skeptical.

"But we aren't now, so we better head in there if you want to see your present," he told her.

Gustavo followed as Beth led the group toward the living room. As soon as she was in sight of the room, she froze with a gasp, and Gustavo, too far back to see, wondered what she was staring at. "David! It's you!" she cried out, running into the room.

Standing in the middle of the room was a tall man wearing a US Navy uniform. He grinned widely at her and held his arms open. By the way she flung herself into him, it was clear that this was the husband she loved so dearly.

"How are you here?" she asked him through tears, and Gustavo noticed that, for once, Beth wasn't holding it together.

"I got a COD to get home two weeks early," he said, holding her tight. "I wanted to be with you and the kids for Christmas."

Beth seemed like she couldn't speak for a good long while, so her father started to explain. "David volunteered for a Carrier Onboard Delivery role, which allowed him to disembark two weeks earlier than the rest of the crew," he told Jeannie and Gustavo.

David nodded. "I'll need to go back in January to make up for this time, but I figured Beth would think the trade-off was worth it," he said.

"When he found out he would be here for Christmas, he contacted me to see if we could do a little something to surprise you," Mr. Lawson said to his daughter, whose face was still buried in her husband's shoulder.

Beth shook with emotion and made some incomprehensible reply, and David grinned, squeezing her tight.

Jeannette wrapped an arm around Gustavo and they watched the tearful reunion, the three children bouncing excitedly around their parents' legs. It was a sweet moment.

"I was expecting a piece of furniture," Beth said at last, making her father laugh.

"Look over by the tree," he said, and as Beth glanced around, Gustavo saw the large chest there that he hadn't noticed before. He guessed the children and their father must have brought it in while the rest of the adults were looking at the bookshelf in the other room.

It also had suncatchers worked into the top of it, and Beth carefully opened the lid.

"Your mom would love it if you used it for your quilting projects," her father suggested quietly.

Beth laughed, wiping the tears from her face. "I guess I will need to start some new quilts soon, then," she said with a happy shrug.

After a few more moments, Beth seemed to come to her senses. "Oh no we're going to be late," she said, looking at the time in alarm. "Jeannie, go get ready right now. Everybody needs to be ready to get out the door in less than half an hour. Let's move," she demanded. She shooed the children out of the room. They seemed to know better than to complain when their mom was in that kind of a mood and rushed to obey, though with a fair amount of pushing and arguing along the way.

Beth looked at her husband in his clean white uniform. "You look perfect," she told him, gazing lovingly up at him.

He looked at her in the same way. "I was told to dress nice," he said.

Beth seemed to approve, because she moved in for another hug.

Jeannie gave Gustavo one last squeeze and ran off to follow her sister's orders. Gustavo watched her go, feeling as if he was in a dream. Then he turned his attention to Angie, who was still in pajamas. He held up the dress he'd brought. "It's time to put this on," he told her.

She did exactly what any toddler would do when there was a time crunch and nice clothes to wear. "I don't wanna!" she said, stomping her foot.

He moved toward her and she started to run away, squealing in delight at this new game, and Gustavo sighed.

Beth unfolded herself from David's arms and knelt

by her. "Angie," she said, her voice firm. "It is time to get dressed. Go to your father right now."

Angie turned and ran to her father, and Gustavo looked up, amazed. "How do you do that?" he asked her.

David said, "She really should have been the one in the military, not me. Beth knows how to give orders better than anyone I've ever met."

Beth turned to him. "You go make sure the kids are putting on nice clothes," she told him, and he winked at Gustavo and left the room.

Between the two adults left, they were able to get Angie dressed and ready. Soon, four children were gathered by the tree, clean and ready to go. Beth looked at them approvingly. "Good. We're all ready to head out the door."

Gustavo and David shared a glance, both trying not to laugh. "Um, Beth," Gustavo said, getting her attention. "Are you going to change?"

Beth looked at her green plaid pajamas in surprise. "I need to get dressed!" she exclaimed, running from the room.

From the hallway, he heard her shout, "I'll be ready in two minutes!" Then in a quieter voice, "Oh Jeannie, you look beautiful!"

Gustavo's stomach twisted in excitement. Jeannie walked into the room, her curls pulled away from her face with only a few tendrils falling down, wearing a silky white dress and little gloves. He was speechless as she came over to him. "What do you think?" she asked.

He finally found his words. "I think you're the most beautiful bride I've ever seen," he answered, touching her cheek.

Angie came over and touched the hem of the dress. "Pretty," she declared.

"So are you," Jeannie said to her. "I love your red dress."

"Auburn dress," Gustavo corrected her with a smirk.

Jeannie put her hands on her hips in mock frustration. "Gustavo Rodriguez, did you pick out a red dress just so you could make that terrible joke on our wedding day?" she asked.

"I really did," he answered, not the least bit chagrined.

She walked over and gave him a kiss.

"None of that, now," Mr. Lawson said as he walked into the room in his suit. "You can kiss at the altar."

Beth ran into the room, breathless and still fixing her hair. "I'm ready," she declared. "Let's get to the church. We've got a wedding to attend."

Gustavo gave Jeannie a grin. "You want to go get married?" he asked her.

"More than anything," she told him. "I love you, Gustavo."

He wrapped his arm around her waist. "I love you, too," he said.

"Okay, but now we're really going to be late,"

Beth said, pushing everyone toward the door. "Boots! Jackets!"

Gustavo helped Jeannie and Angie into their coats and picked up the little girl so she wouldn't be able to splash mud on her dress. Jeannie grasped his free hand, and together they walked out the door, ready to begin their life together as a family.

\* \* \* \* \*

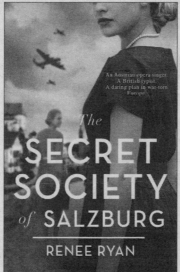

# Get 4 FREE REWARDS!

**We'll send you 2 FREE Books plus 2 FREE Mystery Gifts.**

**FREE**
Value Over
**$20**

Both the **Love Inspired**® and **Love Inspired**® Suspense series feature compelling novels filled with inspirational romance, faith, forgiveness and hope.

**YES!** Please send me 2 FREE novels from the Love Inspired or Love Inspired Suspense series and my 2 FREE gifts (gifts are worth about $10 retail). After receiving them, if I don't wish to receive any more books, I can return the shipping statement marked "cancel." If I don't cancel, I will receive 6 brand-new Love Inspired Larger-Print books or Love Inspired Suspense Larger-Print books every month and be billed just $6.49 each in the U.S. or $6.74 each in Canada. That is a savings of at least 16% off the cover price. It's quite a bargain! Shipping and handling is just 50¢ per book in the U.S. and $1.25 per book in Canada.* I understand that accepting the 2 free books and gifts places me under no obligation to buy anything. I can always return a shipment and cancel at any time by calling the number below. The free books and gifts are mine to keep no matter what I decide.

Choose one: ☐ **Love Inspired**
Larger-Print
(122/322 IDN GRHK)

☐ **Love Inspired Suspense**
Larger-Print
(107/307 IDN GRHK)

Name (please print)

Address                                                                          Apt. #

City                                    State/Province                    Zip/Postal Code

**Email:** Please check this box ☐ if you would like to receive newsletters and promotional emails from Harlequin Enterprises ULC and its affiliates. You can unsubscribe anytime.

### Mail to the Harlequin Reader Service:
**IN U.S.A.:** P.O. Box 1341, Buffalo, NY 14240-8531
**IN CANADA:** P.O. Box 603, Fort Erie, Ontario L2A 5X3

Want to try 2 free books from another series? Call 1-800-873-8635 or visit www.ReaderService.com.

*Terms and prices subject to change without notice. Prices do not include sales taxes, which will be charged (if applicable) based on your state or country of residence. Canadian residents will be charged applicable taxes. Offer not valid in Quebec. This offer is limited to one order per household. Books received may not be as shown. Not valid for current subscribers to the Love Inspired or Love Inspired Suspense series. All orders subject to approval. Credit or debit balances in a customer's account(s) may be offset by any other outstanding balance owed by or to the customer. Please allow 4 to 6 weeks for delivery. Offer available while quantities last.

**Your Privacy**—Your information is being collected by Harlequin Enterprises ULC, operating as Harlequin Reader Service. For a complete summary of the information we collect, how we use this information and to whom it is disclosed, please visit our privacy notice located at corporate.harlequin.com/privacy-notice. From time to time we may also exchange your personal information with reputable third parties. If you wish to opt out of this sharing of your personal information, please visit readerservice.com/consumerschoice or call 1-800-873-8635. **Notice to California Residents**—Under California law, you have specific rights to control and access your data. For more information on these rights and how to exercise them, visit corporate.harlequin.com/california-privacy.

LIRLIS22R3

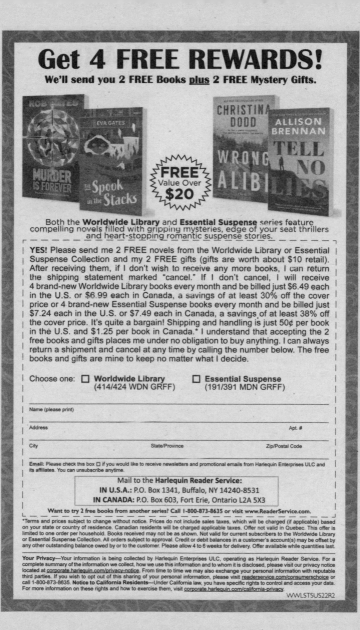

# HARLEQUIN
## PLUS

Try the best multimedia subscription service for romance readers like you!

---

## **Read, Watch and Play.**

Experience the easiest way to get the romance content you crave.

Start your **FREE TRIAL** at
<u>www.harlequinplus.com/freetrial</u>.